the Heart of the City

D0170735

Also by Ron Koertge

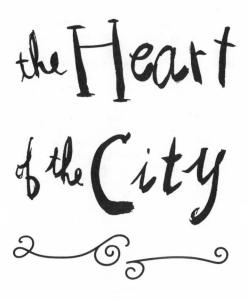

the Heart of the City

RON KOERTGE

ORCHARD BOOKS
New York

CONNETQUOT PUBLIC LIBRARY
760 OCEAN AVENUE
BOHEMIA, NEW YORK 11716

Copyright © 1998 by Ron Koertge
All rights reserved. No part of this book may be reproduced
or transmitted in any form or by any means, electronic or
mechanical, including photocopying, recording or by any
information storage or retrieval system, without permission in writing from the Publisher.

Orchard Books, 95 Madison Avenue, New York, NY 10016

Manufactured in the United States of America
Book design by Mina Greenstein
Decorations by Chris Raschka
The text of this book is set in 12 point New Aster.
1   3   5   7   9   10   8   6   4   2

Library of Congress Cataloging-in-Publication Data

Koertge, Ronald.
The heart of the city / by Ron Koertge.
p.   cm.
Summary: After she and her parents move to an ethnically
mixed inner-city neighborhood, ten-year-old Joy and her
new friend Neesha decide to do something to keep drug
dealers off their block.
ISBN 0-531-30078-1 (trade : alk. paper).—
ISBN 0-531-33078-8 (library)
[1. Inner cities—Fiction.   2. Race relations—Fiction.
3. Afro-Americans—Fiction.   4. City and town life—
Fiction.   5. Friendship—Fiction.]   I. Title.
PZ7.K81825Hg   1998   [Fic]—dc21   97-27856

For my wife, Bianca,
and my friend Jan

June

1

"Boy, do I fit in down here," said Joy. "Me and my blond ponytail."

Her father pulled over to the curb and took some quick pictures of four black men in tank tops standing in front of a beer ad featuring four white men in ski gear. When the first Polaroid was developed, he handed it over the backseat.

"Check this out, Joy. My next painting is right here. I just put the white faces where the black ones are, the black faces where the white ones are, and that's it! Feel the tension in the frame?"

"Not really, but maybe you should ask those guys you just took a picture of, the ones heading right for us. They look tense."

"Gregory." Joy's mom reached to lock all four doors.

"Everything's fine, Melissa."

"Gregory! They don't know you're an artist. You're just a white man with a camera!"

"Dad, c'mon."

As he shot back into traffic, Melissa slumped in her seat. "What are we doing down here, Greg? You did good work in Woodland Hills. The show was a big success."

"Right, but Woodland Hills was temporary; we knew that when we agreed to house-sit. We had to move sometime."

She looked around. "But here of all places."

When Joy heard the sirens she got on her knees and peered out the back window. "If the cops separate us and take us to stinky, slimy interrogation rooms, this is the story: we're lost, we're sorry, we're going right back to Woodland Hills."

"They're not after us, Miss Smarty Pants."

Her dad angled toward the curb. A blue pickup sped by. Right behind it, all dressed up for the chase, came a police car.

Joy's mom tightened her jaw.

Gregory never took his eyes off the busy street. "I didn't pick Ibarra Street, Melissa, okay? It picked me. Anyway, it was dull in Woodland Hills. *I* was dull." He glanced in the rearview mirror. "Weren't you bored, Joy?"

"No. And I already miss Lori."

They stopped for a red light beside a homeless man hauling three grocery carts. But not just any grocery carts; he'd customized these. The engine had rearview mirrors and a hobby horse's head. The caboose had red reflectors and a horse's tail, which was braided into dreadlocks like his own.

Joy's mother just stared. "Oh, my God."

Her father sat up straight. "I've talked to that guy. Ibarra Street has pretty much adopted him. I mean, look how clean he is—he's organized his belongings."

"Broken glass here," said Melissa. "Toxic waste down there."

Joy pointed. "He's got books in that middle cart."

"Good eye, honey! Pass me the camera again, will you?"

Joy's mom put her head in her hands. "Greg, every black person I work with says we're insane to move to the inner city."

"But, Melissa—"

She grabbed his right ear. "You'd better do good work on Ibarra Street, or I'm going to cut this off."

They turned left, cruised past places with names like Resitol Hats, Payless Liquor, Pioneer Chicken, and Muhammad's Mosque of Islam. There were a lot of people on the streets—

bustling here, chatting there, standing or sitting on porches fanning themselves.

He pulled over to the curb again. This time he snapped three or four photos of a storefront.

"Look at all the languages, you guys! Korean, Spanish, I don't know what else. We're going to be bilingual before we know it!"

Joy leaned forward and put her chin on the back of the seat. "Dad? Is there a pool around where we're going? Maybe I could swim when I'm not learning Korean."

"There has to be."

"Oh, sure," said her mother. "In some public park with gang members selling drugs behind the concession stand. No way is she swimming there." She turned around in her seat. "No way," she said to Joy, "are you swimming there."

As they slowed down to make a turn Joy asked, "Are there any kids on Ibarra Street?"

"Of course. Absolutely."

"Like how many?"

"Well, I mean, there's kids everywhere. Right, Melon?"

Melissa gave him The Look. "How many did you actually see, Greg?"

"Yeah, how many, Dad?"

"Some. A few."

"Boys or girls?"

"Both. I saw both."

"How many girls?"

"Uh. Let's see. Well, one, for sure."

That made Joy sit up straight. "Are you kidding? One girl? What if we don't like each other?"

"You only had one friend in Woodland Hills."

"Dad, I picked Lori. We picked each other. Out of a lot of kids."

"I know you and Lori hung out together, but wasn't that pretty much all there was to it? Were you really friends?"

Melissa punched him in the shoulder. "What a thing to say, Greg."

"Yeah, Dad. What a thing to say."

He took both hands off the wheel. "All right, all right. I'm wrong. Not the first time, won't be the last." Then he slowed down. "Put your hands over your eyes," he said. "We're almost there."

Joy glanced at her mother. She shrugged, and they both covered their eyes. Her father had been working on the house for at least three months. Some he did himself. Some he contracted out. But nobody was allowed to see it until it was done. Which was today.

"Now turning onto Ibarra Street, garden spot of Los Angeles." He sounded like a tour guide. "Just a few more— Oh, no!"

Joy peeked. The driveway, *their* driveway, was blocked by a blue pickup. Police cars angled in like the lines on a sundial. Six cops had three kids sitting on the curb with their hands cuffed behind them.

"In Woodland Hills," said Joy, "they have a Welcome Wagon. With little cheeses and coupons for the car wash."

Her father opened the door. She started to get out too.

"Stay, Joy!"

"Woof."

"Sorry, honey." Melissa reached back to pat her. "I mean just wait a minute, okay?"

Her dad talked to one of the officers. He pointed to the big, two-story house. Their house.

It was gray, with white trim, but not gray like an elephant. There was some blue in it, so the house had a kind of light look to it. Lit from inside, sort of. Like a lantern.

Right next door was a vacant lot, weedy but not garbagey. And down from that some smaller houses. Beyond those a brick muffler shop and some more houses. But theirs looked newest.

Two policemen got the boys on their feet and into the backseat of a squad car. A very skinny-looking cop moved the blue truck out of the driveway.

Joy glanced out the side window. The folks who'd been watching the arrest started to watch them. A man with night black hair peered out of a little store called Park's Market. A woman dressed all in white stood with her arms crossed, like she was guarding her yellow house. A man wearing a khaki shirt with an RTD logo on it stood beside a girl in red overalls. So was that her, Joy's only chance for a friend?

Her father leaned into the car. "Everything's fine. No problem. All taken care of. They were very nice."

"They looked like nice criminals," said Joy.

"I meant the police officers."

Up on the porch, he got out his keys with a flourish. He looked at his wife. "I feel like carrying you over the threshold."

"I feel like putting this house on wheels and pushing it back to Woodland Hills."

Then he opened the door. Joy stepped into her new house. She couldn't help herself. "Wow."

It was very cool: high ceilings, varnished floors, and white walls.

Joy watched her mother drift toward the west windows, then mutter, "I don't suppose that these are bullet proof."

"I didn't want," her dad said, "the old this-is-the-kitchen, this-is-the-living-room look." He waved Joy toward him. "This way you can stand at the counter and cut vegetables and still see your friends enjoying themselves."

"My one friend," Joy said. "If I'm lucky." She

looked at the curving staircase. "Is my room up there?"

"Next to the street. With your own bathroom. Then our bedroom and my studio."

"I'm going to take a look, okay?"

Her mother advised her, "The moving van just pulled up. Go get something to carry, okay? It's going to be a long day."

"Don't you want to see the rest of the house?"

"I'll see it soon enough."

Outside, Joy stood off to one side while the guys her dad had hired wrestled some big stuff out of the yellow van. She looked across the street where the girl was standing. Probably that was her father and her grandmother, who was wearing a Chicago Bulls warm-up outfit.

Joy kind of hoped she'd come across and talk. But then maybe she kind of hoped Joy would make the first move. How long would they do that—just look and hope.

So Joy tried a little smile, not one of those I'm-the-neediest-kid-in-the-world-please-love-me leers. Just a neighborly smile. But only Grandma smiled back. Great. Maybe she could hang with her at the Senior Center.

Joy grabbed two lamps and carried them upstairs, right to her room. She could see where her bed would go, so she went over and lay down on the floor where it would be. Out the window was just sky. Nobody would know this was a so-called bad part of town.

Then she heard somebody coming, so she jumped up and looked busy.

It took all afternoon to get things unpacked: beds and black leather couches and Navajo-style rugs, boxes full of pots and pans, clocks and radios, cartons of books, three air conditioners, a dining room table and chairs.

Joy and her mother had labeled dozens and dozens of boxes, so everything flowed from the truck into the house like a river; then it branched off into tributaries that headed for the living room, studio, bedrooms, kitchen, bathrooms.

Joy carried a couple of canvases—*Study in Black & White* and *Untitled #2*—into her dad's studio. Glass ran right up one wall to the ceiling, then, like a skylight, halfway to the pitch. The floor was green indoor-outdoor carpet, as usual. Her dad liked to work barefoot. He also liked to drop paint and spill coffee.

When Joy was sure nobody was looking, she went around and touched all the walls, just for luck. *Her* luck. "Help him work fast, okay?" she whispered. "So we can get out of here."

Joy's room was easy to put together. The movers set her bed and red chest of drawers right where she wanted them. They assembled the metal racks that held the red and white and black and blue bins full of socks and toys and paints and diaries and underwear and tank tops.

When all of that looked pretty good, she made her bed and fluffed up the *Starry Starry Night* comforter. Then her mom came in with new curtains and a footstool. She asked Joy to climb up and hold the brass rods in place.

If Joy peeked out the window, she could see lots of people still on the sidewalk—the family across the street, the people from Park's Market, the lady in white, and a man who could have been somebody's grandpa. He was dressed in black slacks and a dress shirt and he stood beside this classy-looking old car. Everybody looked at her family's house, then at one another, then at the house again.

Joy's mother eyed the curtains from across the room. She dashed up to move them an inch or two, then leaned on the wall. She pushed some blond hair back out of her face, sighed, and plunged both hands into the back pockets of her farmer-style overalls.

Then she motioned for Joy to come away from the window and sit beside her. "For a while," she said. "I want you to be extra careful. I don't think anybody wants to hurt you. I just—*we* just—don't know the rules yet. Like in Woodland Hills and those rules about gas-powered leaf blowers, remember?"

"Uh-huh."

"Well, I'm sure there are rules here too. Not about gas-powered leaf blowers, probably. But other things."

Joy tugged at the neck of her PICASSO sweatshirt. "I'm always careful."

"Don't talk to strangers."

"Mom, we just moved here. Everybody's a stranger."

"You know what I mean."

"Sure, those guys Deputy Dawg warns you about."

"It's much more dangerous than in Woodland Hills. *Much*. More than half the calls I get at work are from right around here." Melissa slid one arm around Joy's shoulder and leaned into her. "Are you going to be okay?" she asked.

Joy shrugged. "I guess, but why do we have to do what Dad wants all the time? I mean, there's three of us. Why didn't we vote? If we'd voted, I'd still see Lori every day. I could still go swimming."

Melissa kissed her on the part in her hair. "Your father isn't like most people."

"No kidding."

"I knew that when I married him." She smiled. "Actually it's one of the reasons I married him. And it's not that his work is more important than me or you, but it is very important to him. *Very*."

"It still doesn't seem fair."

"I know. And I don't blame you for being upset. Not many people move to the heart of the city anymore, much less white people."

Joy stood up and walked to the window. She sighed. "So if this is the heart of the city, is its head in the ocean or is it soaking its feet?"

Melissa stood up. "You're more like your father all the time."

Joy felt her upper lip. "I hope that doesn't mean I'll have a mustache someday."

Her mother grinned as Joy pushed her new camel-print curtains back and forth. Then she put her face against the cool glass and mashed her nose flat. "Can I go across the street and talk to that girl?"

"Tomorrow, okay?"

"Mom, if I have to be locked up in the house forever and never go swimming again for as long as I live, I at least need somebody to play with."

"Let's just take it easy our first day here." She held out one hand. "Now, c'mon. I helped you with your room, you help me with ours."

SETTING UP THINGS and arranging them stopped being fun. Around five o'clock the movers just put the last of the stuff in the center of the living room and clocked out. A couple of hours later Joy and her folks pretty much collapsed. They slumped at the new table in the new kitchen and ate a new pizza.

Gregory looked toward the living room.

"I like seeing our old stuff again," he said. "It held up pretty good in storage."

Joy took a drink of root beer. "It was too weird sitting on somebody else's sofa and sleeping in somebody else's bed. I was always afraid I was going to spill something."

"House-sitting *was* peculiar," Gregory said. "But the money we saved not paying rent helped us buy this place."

Joy's mom yawned. "I don't know about the rest of you, but I feel like I carried that refrigerator on my back all the way from Woodland Hills." She stretched and stood up. "Let's go to bed. Greg, did you lock up?"

"Uh-huh."

"Are you sure?"

"Melissa. Will you relax? I locked up. I checked the alarm system. I'm not going to run around checking everything twice. We're not under siege here, okay?"

Joy pushed back her chair. "Is this going to be a tussle, a fracas, a fight, or a battle?"

"Don't sass me, Joy," her mother warned. "Not tonight."

"You're the one who bought me the thesaurus, Mom. I wanted a pony."

"Joy! Go to bed."

She climbed the stairs, then—halfway up—looked back. She knew it wasn't polite to listen in, but . . .

"Don't tell me," her mother said, "that we're not under siege. We're trapped here, Greg. We can't get out; our friends aren't going to drive down to see us."

"What friends are those?"

"Well, your friends: Morry, Leslie, Charles—other painters. Or my friends from work."

Joy saw her father frown and lean across the table. "Your friends from work? The same ones who never came to Woodland Hills?"

"Well, they're busy. Everybody's busy."

They're at it again, thought Joy. She'd heard this argument a dozen times in the last couple of months: what friends they did and didn't have and which ones would they lose or never even make because they were moving to the ghetto.

Joy's mom took a long drink of water. "Well, but *we* can't even go out anymore. Rochelle's son drew us a map. It shows what streets you can take in the daytime to keep from stumbling onto somebody's precious turf."

"So? We take those streets."

"At night, you can't go anywhere!"

"Where did we ever go at night?"

"But now we couldn't if we wanted to."

"But we don't want to. We never have."

Joy's mother shot up from the table. Joy inched forward so she could see her. "I worry all the time."

"I worry too."

"Not as much."

"I'm used to Ibarra Street. It's all new to you. Give it a chance, Melissa. I think we'll make friends here. I really do."

Joy's dad got up then, crossed the tile floor, and put his arms around his wife. Joy had seen enough, so she went on upstairs.

Her folks were pretty good about fighting. Nobody had to win. They just both said what was on their minds. Lori's parents "never fought." Oh, sure. Just walking in that house could give Joy a stomachache. No, she liked fighting out loud better.

Everything in her bathroom worked, so that was cool. And it was cool to lie in her old bed in her new room. It really had been weird living in somebody else's house. The Arteburns had a daughter too, so Joy got her room. But it was way too girly—like all those expensive dolls locked up in glass cases, so they looked like specimens. Test-tube dollies. Joy couldn't play with them, just admire them. What good was that?

Joy lay on her left side, then her right. She turned the pillow over. She turned crossways. But every sound made her jump. All she ever heard about the heart of the city was how dangerous it could be. About who got shot, mostly. Usually by mistake. According to the news, there were bullets flying all over the place.

But she hadn't seen any guns. Nobody looked scared. Nobody had scars or bandages. Nobody looked mean, just curious.

But maybe the really mean people only come out after midnight or something? Maybe they keep track of where the ten-year-old kids lived. Especially the new kids. Especially the new white kids.

Oh, man! Joy said to herself, sitting straight up in bed.

HER DAD MOVED A CEREAL BOX and looked at the wooden bowl of fruit in the center of the table. "I could never paint a still life," he said. "Not in art school. Not now."

Joy reached for a banana. "Did you guys hear somebody on the roof last night?"

Her mother was standing at the counter, dressed for work in ambulance colors: red blouse, white pants. She turned and looked at her husband. "I didn't sleep a wink, Greg. Not one wink."

"I'm pretty sure there were like ten people on the roof. People with fangs."

Her father stretched. "I didn't hear anything." He looked at Joy. "And certainly not on the roof."

"And it sounded like blood was dripping off their fangs and gurgling down the gutters."

Her dad shook his spoon at her. "Stop scaring your mother."

"Well, I don't have any friends anymore, so I have to scare somebody."

"Are you going to work today, Greg?"

He nodded. "I'm going to try, Mel. The studio's a mess. I can at least get that in some kind of shape."

Melissa put down her fork. "Promise me, while I'm gone, you won't let Joy out of your sight."

"Melon, nothing's going to happen. Come here."

He led her through the house. Their heels clicked on the hardwood floor. Joy followed, ducked under her father's arm, and surfaced between them.

Through the window, she watched cars and trucks drive by, moving in spurts. She saw a boy in a wide-brimmed straw hat pushing a white cart-on-wheels. Someone taped a sign on the window of Park's Market. Across the street, four men played cards. One of them looked like the man who'd been standing by the girl. The only other girl for miles.

Joy thought that maybe Ibarra Street wasn't so bad in the daytime. It was alive, anyway, compared to Woodland Hills, which had been super quiet. The whole place under glass, sort of. Like those dolls.

"I love this street," said her father. "It's got energy to burn."

"Don't say *burn*." Melissa picked up her lunch as Joy leaned for a good-bye kiss. Then her mom said, "Straight down Ibarra to Gaviota. Turn right there, two blocks to the freeway. Right? And of course, all four doors locked and eyes straight ahead."

Joy and her father stood in the doorway and watched the old blue Volvo pull out of the driveway.

He put one arm around her shoulders, and she leaned into him. "Your mom's just worried. Mostly about you, but me too. And herself. And the house. You know."

"Uh-huh."

He kissed her on top of the head. "Are you still mad?"

"A little."

"I probably would be too, if I were you."

"So why did we move?"

"I'm so unhappy when my work doesn't go well."

"But, Dad. Now I'm unhappy and so is Mom!"

Gregory frowned and smoothed his brown hair. He wiped both hands on his paint-splattered pants. "Before you were born, your mother and I talked about priorities, you know? About what's important and what's not so important.

When you get married, you and your husband will have one of those talks too."

"No kidding. That way *I'll* be the one who always gets her way."

"It seems like that, I know. But my work is separate from me, kind of. It's like there's four of us in the family."

"But it gets a vote, doesn't it? That's why it's like you and it against me and Mom, and you and it always win."

Her father frowned. "I just want to try Ibarra Street. I think we'll like it. If we don't or if it gets dangerous, we are out of here."

"Great. I saw a house on the freeway once, like on a big skateboard? That's what we'll do. We'll take this one with us!"

"Let's not get ahead of ourselves, sweetheart. Give Ibarra Street a chance."

Joy opened the door and peeked out. "How far are we from the ocean?"

"Not very. Eight, maybe ten miles."

"It's cooler here, anyway."

"In every sense of the word." Gregory rubbed his hands together. "Would you mind going to the market? We could use some milk."

"Go to the market alone? I thought you promised Mom you wouldn't let me out of your sight."

"I can see you from here."

She glanced down the street. "That little place is the market, right?"

"Mr. and Mrs. Park own it. I used to buy Cokes and beer and things for the carpenters. Introduce yourself. They know who you are. I showed them your picture."

Next door to the market was a shoe repair shop. "Who owns that?"

"I don't know. The last thing I wanted to do was rush around the whole neighborhood with my big white hand out. So I took it easy."

"Just milk?"

"Uh-huh."

She wiped her palms on her jeans. "Now?"

"Please."

Joy tucked a few dollar bills in her pocket, went outside and down the steps. Without turning around she called out, "You're watching, right?"

"Right."

She held up one hand. "How many fingers?"

"Three."

"Okay, but don't zone out and start thinking about a painting."

At the corner, a car cruised up to the light. It was so low to the ground that it looked like it was sneaking around. A window on the passenger's side slid down, and a man leaned out. He had a shaved head and big gold chains around his neck.

Joy stepped back. Her heart started to beat fast and hard. She was breathing through her mouth. Panting.

Then he spit.

When the car pulled away, she turned around. Her dad had gone inside. Was he watching from in there? Was that his face in the window?

Half a block away the man she'd seen yesterday, the one in black slacks standing by his special car, got out of the front seat and started her way. He wore the same clothes, or maybe the same kind of clothes. Every little hair—and there weren't that many of them—was in its place, like children lying down at nap time.

Joy stopped, then retreated a step or two. She could hear her mother: *Don't talk to strangers.*

"I'm Franco Lossi," he rasped.

She looked around. Two boys dribbled basketballs. The lady in white peered into her mailbox, then at Joy. Cars and trucks crept by. It wasn't like she was all alone. "I'm Joy Fontaine."

He looked toward the corner. "I saw what just happened. They do that sometimes."

"Black people spit at you?"

"Young men. It's nothing to worry about. It's not personal."

A station wagon honked its horn, and they both turned. A black man—really bald this time, not like the guy with the gold chains—smiled and waved. Mr. Lossi waved back. "My barber," he explained. Then he motioned toward his Oldsmobile. "Have you ever seen a classic car?"

Joy looked over: blue and white without a nick or a ding. The chrome shot across the sides like bolts hurled by one of those Greek gods. In the perfect hubcaps, Joy could see the whole world reflected.

He opened the door. "Do you want to sit in the driver's seat?"

Joy's mother had told her never to do that. Not in Woodland Hills, not anyplace, not ever.

"No, thank you."

Mr. Lossi stared into the distance. "With so many people leaving, I thought I'd never see another young family come to Ibarra. I watched the three of you move in yesterday, and I saw the old days." He pointed. "Fifty years ago there was a restaurant called Roma Gardens right where that muffler shop is now. Everybody who lived here was Italian. For a long time, if an Italian family moved out, an Italian family moved in. Now we're what's called a rainbow neighborhood."

"Does that mean there's a pot of gold some-place?" asked Joy.

"Maybe right here."

Joy looked around her: the weedy vacant lot, the houses that needed paint, old cars sagging at the curb.

Yeah, right, she thought. It sure looks like I'm

standing in a pot of gold. "I should probably get Dad's milk."

Mr. Lossi smiled, leaned down, and whispered, "If there's ever any kind of trouble, come and see me. I'm retired, but I still know a few people."

"Can these people make guys in cars stop spitting at me?"

"That's really too small a problem for them."

"Can they convince my dad to move back to Woodland Hills?"

"That's really too personal for them."

"Can I arrange to have my math teacher's legs broken?"

Mr. Lossi smiled. "You've been seeing too many movies."

"Bye, Mr. Lossi."

The inside of Park's Market was cool and dim. And small! The cans and bottles looked small too, the kind of thing you'd buy if you lived by yourself or didn't have very much money. A boy with a cool ponytail was standing with his mom. She glanced at her list and pointed. "Paco," she said. "Colgate."

Col-gah-tay—Joy loved that! Toothpaste from Mexico.

She grinned at the boy, who was only a couple of years older than she, but he just looked around her, not at her. The way a knife thrower will outline his partner.

"Paco. *Por favor!*"

"God, Mom," he hissed. "Speak English!" Then he turned his hat around so the bill was pointing backward and stalked out of the store.

When Joy got to the dairy case, she reached in and took out a carton of nonfat.

Suddenly a woman charged out of the back room. Joy jumped and almost dropped her milk. "Oh, you are here at last!"

This had to be Mrs. Park. Did she count as a stranger? She was sure dressed strange in a *Phantom of the Opera* sweatshirt, green jeans, and bright orange flip-flops. She reached for Joy's hand.

"Miss," she said, pumping hard. "Come to the counter. Come."

Joy followed her back to the cash register. It was surrounded by miniature bleachers full of candy and gum. On the wall behind those was a lot of whiskey and gin. It was locked up, like it was being punished.

"I am Mrs. Park. This is husband, Young."

"He looks pretty young," said Joy politely.

Mrs. Park laughed. "No, no. Young his name."

He smiled and offered a candy bar.

Joy shook her head. "Thanks, but my mom doesn't let me eat candy."

"Very beautiful young lady. Beautiful hair. Beautiful form. Where your father?"

Beautiful form? Joy blushed. "Thank you,

thanks. Uh, Dad's, you know, home. So, uh, how much is the milk?"

"Nothing! A gift!" Mrs. Park pushed the carton into her hands like it was hot. "Welcome."

"Oh, no. Really. I couldn't." Joy fumbled in her pocket, laid two dollars on the counter. "Take this, please."

She backed out of the store, waving and, for some reason, bowing too.

Her father was leaning against the wall outside. When he tapped her on her shoulder, she jumped.

"God, Dad, where were you when they were spitting at me?"

"The Parks spit at you?"

"No. That guy in the car."

"Oh, him." He tugged at Joy's faded T-shirt, straightening it. He reached for the milk. "That wasn't personal."

"That's what Mr. Lossi said."

"I saw you talking to him."

"I thought you'd abandoned me. I thought this had turned into something like one of those wilderness things—on my own with just a match and a pocketknife and a big yellow dog."

"I was still watching."

"Mr. Lossi asked me if I wanted to sit in his car, and I said no."

"Good girl. What else did he say?"

"Just that he lived here fifty years. We've never lived anywhere even fifty months!"

"We did too. That time I had the studio downtown by Al's Bar. But you were really little."

"I remember that. I liked the skylight."

"Good for you. Good sense-memory." He slipped his arm around her. "Let's go home. I need to get some work done."

Joy pointed. "If we walk that way, we could go by that girl's house, the one I saw yesterday."

They cruised toward a shoe repair shop that exhaled as they passed, its breath like leather and polish. They studied the hairstyles displayed in the window of Miriam's Beauty Nook and read the sticker that said ALLAH IS GREAT. Then Joy and her father passed a green house, a blue one, and a smaller one that was turquoise.

"That's a nice touch," her dad said. "It looks like a momma house and a pappa house got together and had a baby." He glanced at her. "Remember on the color charts how green and blue make—"

"You're really something, Dad. Every other father in the world is having this sit-down, heart-to-heart talk with his kid about drugs and guns, but you're pointing to the mamma house and the pappa house."

"Tell me you love me, anyway."

"I might. For a dollar."

"You drive a hard bargain for a ten-year-old."

"I'll hold your hand for free."

It was nice strolling along with her father. And it was nice seeing other people and trucks and stuff. Woodland Hills had been pretty quiet.

Then a carful of young men drove by and glared at them, so Joy moved closer to her dad.

"Try and remember," said Gregory, "that the black people you see on TV—MTV in your case—aren't all the black people."

"Yeah? Well those guys were right off the front of one of those CDs I'm not old enough to buy."

"When I was their age, I wanted to look tough too. I had a leather jacket."

She looked up at her father. "No way."

"Absolutely. Wore the collar up and everything."

"Have you still got it?"

He shook his head. "Gave it away when I got married."

Joy groaned. "Lori had a leather jacket. It was pink and had Pocahontas on the back, but it was still leather."

He mussed her hair. "Tell you what. The first painting I sell from Ibarra Street, I'll buy you one. A black one. But don't tell your mom."

They paused at the house across the street from theirs, the house with the cardplayers on the front porch.

"Her father's a bus driver," Gregory said. "Mr. Park told me. Maybe he's working."

The yard had an iron fence, but it was too low to keep anything out except maybe a crazed hamster. The fence was white and looked like somebody had just painted it. The lawn was neat and green.

Joy's father stepped through the gate. No one on the porch looked up. Three men sat back in their chairs and stared at their cards. Joy noticed that their shirts were green, blue, and turquoise. Just like the houses down the block. She was glad her father didn't have his camera.

"Knock, knock," Gregory said.

Nothing. Nobody looked up.

"She was here yesterday," Joy whispered, "but now . . ."

"Well, let's just say we tried. There'll be another time."

They'd just turned away when the screen door opened and a man asked, "Can I help you?" The girl, *that* girl, slipped out behind him. She had on orange shorts and a T-shirt with a gold star on it.

"Oh yes. Hi. Well, we're . . ." Gregory pointed. "We just moved in across the way there, and I thought I should . . ." He put his hand on Joy's shoulder. "We thought *we* should say hello."

"C'mon up."

Joy watched the other girl drift in behind one of the men playing cards as her father shook hands.

"I'm Walter Kincaid. This is my daughter, Neesha. These big-time gamblers are Mr. Aliju-won, Mr. Pickett, and Mr. Jardin."

The cardplayers sort of laid their hands in Gregory's and made him do all the shaking. Then the middle one folded his cards, sat back, and looked right at him.

"You down here because we exotic, my friend?"

"No."

"This your way of showin' your pals that you the most liberal?"

"No."

"I hope to God that you don't think you're some kind of model for troubled inner-city youth."

"Not at all."

Neesha drifted toward the porch swing. She hopped into it, pushed herself, looked down at the seat beside her. So Joy wandered over, turned around at just the right time so the swing caught her behind her knees, and plopped down beside Neesha.

"Exactly what are you doin' here?" asked Mr. Jardin.

Joy took in his sharp little mustache, sharp crease in his white slacks, shoes with pointy toes. "Who's he?" she whispered.

"Owns some liquor stores."

"I'm just looking," said Gregory, "for a congenial place to paint."

"Your dad's a painter?" asked Neesha. "Pictures and stuff?"

"Uh-huh."

"You an artist too?"

"I wish."

"Have you got any brothers and sisters?"

"No. You?"

"Uh-uh."

Joy's dad pointed over his shoulder. "I just sort of fell in love with the house," said Gregory. "There's some beautiful craftsmanship in there."

Mr. Alijuwon took a sip of coffee. "I remember the beautiful people livin' there. They so beautiful, we had to call the police."

"Is he your real dad?" asked Neesha.

"Sure."

"Mine too."

When her father took a step backward, Joy slipped out of the swing. "See you," she said, then went and stood on the second step.

Neesha's father uncrossed his muscular arms and smiled. "Well, welcome to the neighborhood." Then he held out his hand. But the pointy man threw down his cards, shot to his feet, and shook his finger.

"Black and white are never gonna get along.

There's too much history, too much bad blood. You hear me? We ain't never gonna get along."

There was a long quiet couple of seconds. Everybody looked someplace else.

Then Neesha asked, "Hey, do you have skates?"

Joy nodded.

"Me too. Maybe we could skate sometime."

3

NEXT MORNING Gregory stopped eating Special K long enough to wave his spoon. "So they weren't all that friendly, but they were gorgeous, weren't they, Joy?"

"Neesha's pretty."

He grabbed Melissa's sleeve as she passed. "Melon, all you ever hear is black people this and black people that. Nobody ever talks about the complexity of the spectrum. From left to right they were a perfect color chart: raw umber, burnt Siena, burnt umber, and Naples yellow hue."

Joy's mother looked at her and cringed. "He didn't say that, did he?"

She shook her head. "But I wasn't listening to everything. I was talking to Neesha."

Gregory headed for the refrigerator. "They were still gorgeous. Everybody in Woodland Hills was so white."

"She's got skates too."

Mom kissed Joy on the part in her hair. "These men weren't hostile, were they, honey?"

"I guess not."

Gregory nodded. "I'm just the new guy. They were sure no worse than that man next door in Woodland Hills. I walk over and say, 'Hi, I'm your new neighbor, and I'm a painter.' He takes one look at me and says, 'We've already got a handyman.' "

Melissa looked out the kitchen window, leaning so that she could see the street. "Who's the old Italian in the Oldsmobile? He's there when I leave; he's there when I come home."

"That's Franco Lossi. He's always in his car, kind of a one-man Neighborhood Watch, I think."

Just then the doorbell chimed. Melissa jumped and put her hand over her heart. As Joy ran, she warned her, "Look first!"

There stood Neesha and the lady Joy had seen before. This time she had on white athletic shoes and a purple-and-gold Los Angeles Lakers' warm-up outfit.

"This is my grandma," Neesha said. "Her name is Mrs. Kincaid." Then she held out a pie.

Joy led them into the kitchen. Gregory sho. to his feet. Melissa wiped her fingers on a tea towel before she shook hands, then pulled out two chairs.

Mrs. Kincaid looked around the kitchen and smiled. She smiled at the kitchen stove and refrigerator, she smiled at the jars of oatmeal and rice, and the blue bowl full of eggs. She felt the leaves of the ficus tree that stood beside the door and buried her face in a big amaryllis like it was an oxygen mask. Finally she said, "You all have performed a miracle here. This place was a hazard."

"My dad did it all," Joy said.

Mrs. Kincaid stared at him. "*You* did this?"

"Some of it. But, please, don't tell those card-players."

"Oh, don't pay any attention to those sour-puss Blues Brothers. You're welcome here. I would have been on your front porch sooner, but one of my friends from church is poorly." She nodded at the cup of coffee Melissa sat in front of her. "I'm either an old lady with a heart as big as all outdoors," she said. "Or a busy-body who can't keep her nose out of other people's business."

"Well," Gregory said, "I'm either an artist with a restless spirit, or somebody who didn't know a good thing when he had it."

smiled. "Then you and I should

ugged at her grandmother's sleeve.
and I go skating?"

can, child. But I can't speak for Mrs.
Fo.. .ine."

They looked at Melissa, who said, "But not in
the street."

"No, ma'am."

"And not on the sidewalk if there are people."

"Yes, ma'am." Joy caught Neesha's eye.

"And not on anybody's property."

They said it together. "No, ma'am."

"I know, I know. You both think I'm crazy."

"Yes, ma'am."

Neesha followed Joy upstairs. The skylight let
in a long, hot column of sun that slashed across
the high, white walls.

"This is nice. I've got bars on my bedroom
window," Neesha said.

"Do you ever have to get in the bathtub or
on the floor because bullets are flying everywhere?"

She shook her head. "Not on Ibarra Street,
but I know kids who do."

Neesha touched the TV and VCR. She petted
the Van Gogh bedspread, flipped through a
couple of books, and peeked into some of the
Crayola-colored bins that held most of Joy's

stuff. Then she asked, "Can I see some of your dad's pictures?"

"Sure, come on."

They crossed the hall together and slipped into the studio. Neesha looked around. She put up one hand and stopped a ray of sun. "This is great, girl!" She grabbed a piece of yellow chalk from an old enamel-topped table and made two wide slashes in the air.

Then Joy pointed. "Here's some of his stuff."

Neesha cruised past the canvases leaning against the wall. She read their names out loud. "*Auntie Violence, Melon Collie Baby, Big Brown Painting.* Well, at least I got that last one."

"Yeah. It's a big brown painting."

Neesha gestured. "This one here looks like he spilled something."

"He let a brush kinda dry out, then he dribbled paint off it."

"Man, this art looks easy. In school we had to draw a horse."

"Did you?"

"Draw one? Sure."

"Mine looked like a squirrel. An ugly squirrel."

As Joy led Neesha back across the hall she asked, "Are you smart?"

"Pretty smart."

Joy ducked into the closet, then backed out with her skates. She turned them over and ran one hand across the wheels. "School's hard for me," she admitted.

"It's hard for me too," said Neesha. "Sometimes, anyhow."

"But you just said you were smart."

"But that doesn't mean school's easy. Anyway, I think it's like when my dad goes to the gym. He says, 'No pain, no gain.' School's supposed to be a little hard."

Downstairs, Joy thanked Mrs. Kincaid for the pie and kissed her folks.

"You know, Mom," she said, juggling her helmet and knee pads, "if Neesha and I can't skate on the street or the sidewalk or on anybody's property, that only leaves the roof."

"Oh yeah. Thanks for reminding me. No skating on the roof, either."

Mrs. Kincaid assured Joy's mother that the playground down the way was safe. "All of Ibarra Street is safe."

They left by the front door, crossed the street, and went up the walk that led to Neesha's house.

Inside, it was cool and dim and smelled like apple pie.

"Does your dad like driving a bus?" asked Joy.

"It's okay."

"Does your grandma work?"

"Yeah, but not for money. She just helps people."

In the living room was a wide-armed sofa and chairs that made Joy want to sit in them. There were lots of pictures of Jesus on the walls, and a china cabinet with gold-edged plates. Joy had to turn sideways to squeeze past the coatrack and the steamer trunk in the hall.

"I like your house. All my dad likes is space. Mom wants to hang something up and he says, 'There's already something up on that wall: light.'"

She sat on Neesha's bed, right below the poster of Maya Angelou.

"Man, have you got a lot of books!"

"Yeah. Grandma wouldn't let me go outside at night at all until last year. And I still can't go very far. So she made sure I had lots to read."

Joy pointed to the television set and VCR. "Do you watch TV?"

"Five hours a week is all. You?"

"Hour a day."

"So what do you watch?"

Joy looked down at the red bedspread. "Don't laugh, okay? I like The Weather Channel."

"Really? *I* like The Weather Channel. That looks like a good job." Neesha jumped up and pointed to a map on the wall. "See," she said. "I already got that index finger part down."

On the bottom shelf of one bookcase were all kinds of dolls. They weren't under glass, either. They looked like they'd been played with a lot.

Neesha backed out of her closet, dragging her skates. "C'mon."

On their way through the living room, Joy stopped in front of a table loaded down with photographs, all in silver frames. There was Neesha in a stiff white dress graduating from kindergarten, Neesha wearing a purple robe posing with the children's choir, Neesha wearing mouse ears and hugging Snow White at Disneyland, Neesha and her father and a tall woman wearing glasses and a green-and-gold African-style dress.

Joy pointed. "Is this your mom?"

Neesha nodded. "She died last year."

"Oh, man. Did she get shot?"

Neesha wasn't wearing her skates yet; she was holding them, letting them swing. Back and forth they went, like a pendulum. They ticked off five long seconds before she said, "What do you think? All black people who die get shot?"

Joy didn't know where to look. Not at Neesha, not at the picture of Neesha's mom, not even at a bowl of candy corn. She turned red all over. Under her socks, under her clothes. Even her hands were embarrassed.

"I'm sorry, Neesha."

"I'd pop you with this skate, but then you'd say all black kids are violent."

"I would not."

"I'm about the last person you ought to disrespect. You need me, girl."

"Why do I need you?"

" 'Cause you don't know nothin' about nothin'."

"I do too."

"Not about livin' down here, you don't."

Joy let her voice drop. "Oh."

"Yeah, I'd say 'Oh.' " Neesha threw her skates on the couch, where they bounced and clattered.

Joy looked down at her shoes, which seemed bigger and whiter than usual. "Do you want me to go home?" she asked.

Neesha took a deep breath and let it out. Then another. "Don't go on my account."

"You sure?"

"Yeah, my grandma doesn't let me carry on very long. I either take a couple of deep breaths and that's that, or I have to go to my room."

"Even if it's not your fault?"

"Grandma says if it's not my fault, why get mad at all?"

"When my mom and I fight, and then one of us is sorry, we play It Never Happened."

Neesha reached for her skates. "So you just start all over?"

"Right. She like goes out of the room and comes back in again."

"Does it work?"

"Uh-huh."

"So which one of us goes out of this room?"

"Me." She stepped back into the hall, knocked politely, peered around the door. "Hello, I'm new here. I'm Joy Fontaine. I think you'll like me because I'm really nice and I never say the wrong thing."

Neesha held out her hand. "How do you do, I'm Neesha Kincaid."

"I heard that you like to skate."

Neesha laughed. "You heard right."

Carrying their stuff, the girls headed down the street, south this time, away from Mr. Lossi in his car and the Park's Market. For a while, Joy tagged along behind Neesha. Then she drew even with her.

"How long can you stay out today?" she asked. It still took a little effort to sound natural.

Neesha just looked at her. "What?"

"How long can we skate? You know, do you have to go to dance class or something?"

"I don't go to dance class or anything else. I just do what I want."

"My friend Lori always had to go someplace. Her mom used to call my mom and make an appointment for us to play."

Neesha almost grinned. "An appointment to play? Are you kidding?"

"She was in a class for everything."

"No way. How old was she?"

"Ten."

"Wow. Did you do that?"

Joy shook her head. "I used to swim at the Y though."

"There used to be a pool a couple of blocks from here. But somebody got shot behind the snack stand, so nobody goes to that park anymore."

"There's all kinds of little parks in Woodland Hills, but nobody goes there, either."

"Gangs?"

"No. Everybody's got their own barbecue and their own backyard."

"Big yards?"

"Yeah."

They walked without saying anything for half a block or so.

"Is there really a lot of stuff I have to know down here?" Joy asked.

"Some. I was just mad before. Mostly, you just watch my back and I watch yours."

Just then a car pulled up beside them. It was an old Pontiac, packed full of boys. The radio was up high; its speakers sounded fuzzy. "Yo, Oreos."

"Don't look," hissed Neesha. "Just keep walkin'."

The boy on the passenger's side stuck both arms out the window. "Hey, Ebony and Ivory!"

Neesha picked up the pace and, when they reached the playground, ducked into the first entrance. When the car sped away, she said to Joy, "You all right?"

"Uh-huh."

"You just look whiter than usual is all."

"They scared me a little."

"Well, you gotta be ice with boys like that, okay? Just freeze 'em out. They ever stop you and you have to talk? Get right in their face. You're tougher than they are."

Joy looked toward the street. "I don't feel tougher."

"Hey, they're just actin'. You act too."

They sat down on a bench and laced up their skates. Joy kept glancing toward the entrance to the playground.

"Were those kids in the car gang members?"

"No."

Joy read the wall, decorated with graffiti: 19 STREET, DOG TOWN, TOMB DUMMIES.

"Are those gangs?" she asked.

Neesha shook her head. "Just taggers."

Joy got up, making her skates into a T so she could stand still for a second. "Why is that last one crossed out?"

"It's like a game: I write my sign, you x it out and write yours, I come back and x yours. Trouble is they get tired of that and start callin' each other out."

"But they don't belong to a gang? I thought—"

"The only real gangs are about money, not who crossed whose name out the most."

"Money?"

"Drug money mostly. That's why they shoot at each other. Somebody's trying to move into somebody else's territory. And that's why you got to be careful, 'cause all these shoot-outs are about is drugs or turf or both. They don't care about kids like us, but you sure don't want to get in their way. They're not real good shots, so they just shoot a lot."

Joy looked around. "Is it dangerous where we are now?"

"Ibarra Street's always been a good place. But up a ways it's bad, like on Nasty Street. And there's other places you shouldn't go. I'll tell you all that."

"Is Nasty Street its real name?"

She shook her head. "Nasturtium. But every-body calls it Nasty Street now."

Joy pointed to half a dozen kids playing bas-ketball. They all seemed to be wearing extrabig, extragadgety shoes. Their tank tops hung almost to their knees.

"What about those guys."

"They're cool. Grandma knows all of 'em. If they come over, just say, 'Sup, due.' "

Sure enough, the boys started eyeing them, leaning in, whispering. One darted back and shot from outside the paint. Another one drove hard with the rebound. Pretty soon they came over.

Joy watched them swagger.

"Too many old Michael Jackson videos," Neesha whispered, and they both snickered.

"What's so funny?" demanded the leader.

"Nothin'," said Neesha.

"So you laughin' at nuthin'?"

"We not botherin' you, Cornell. Go play ball."

Cornell looked Joy up and down. "What you doin' down here, girl?"

"Sup, due," she said.

"You new from the house on the corner, ain't you. I heard bout you."

Neesha stepped in front of her. "So now you know everything. You Master of the Universe, okay? You go on *Jeopardy*, ain't no way you not winnin' everything, you know what I'm sayin'? So leave us alone now."

Cornell sneered. He pulled the black bandanna lower on his forehead. "You think you bettern us, anyways. Now wid dis one here, you really think you bettah."

"I might want to *do* better, Cornell. But I sure don't think I'm better than you could be."

"Now you soundin' like yo granma."

Neesha shrugged. "So?"

Cornell signaled to his buddies. "Well, we be watchin' you," he said. "Both of you."

When they were all the way back to their court, Joy asked, "How do you do that?"

"How do I do what?"

"Talk different like you did to those boys."

"Oh. I can teach you, if you want."

"Like talking French."

Neesha coasted in a tight circle. "This is a lot easier than that." She scratched her head. "Let's see. Well, always say *axe* and *hep*."

Joy threw back her shoulders. "Hep me with dat axe."

Neesha grinned. "No, no. *Axe* means *ask*. And *with* is *wif*." She glanced at a lady tugging at her German shepherd. "Like, 'Hep me wif dis po dog.' "

"Oh, okay. I got it."

"And for sure use this: 'Know what I'm sayin'?' "

"I know that one."

"Good, so say that and hold your hands like this." She stuck out her index finger, little finger, and thumb. She tucked the other two in. "And kind of wave your hands around." Neesha started to sway. "You know what I'm sayin'? You know what I'm sayin'?"

Joy started to sway too. "Basketball be playin', you know what I'm sayin'?"

Neesha shook her head. "Uh-uh. That basketball ain't playin' itself." She pointed. "Now, those boys be playin'. Okay?" She pointed at her jeans.

"Like these pants be frayin', you know what I'm sayin'?"

Joy frowned. "So dem fields need hayin'?"

"That's it! And them chickens be layin'."

They stopped to laugh. Neesha bumped Joy with her hip, and leaned into her.

"Them waiters be trayin'," Joy said.

"Them cowards betrayin'."

"Nice one." She pointed toward her house and Neesha's. "Your grandma be prayin'."

"Mr. Park be weighin'."

"The florist bouquetin'."

"That car Chevroletin'."

"The movie matineein'."

"New Mexico Santa Fein'."

It was too much. They fell back on the bench, shrieking.

"That was cool," said Neesha when she'd recovered. "But keep that to yourself around my dad, okay? He'll say we sound like project girls. Tells me to forget that stuff 'cause in the real world money talks and it don't sound like that." She grinned. "It's still kind of cool when your folks don't know what you're sayin' though. My friend Tanasha and I used to talk trash a lot, but she moved."

"Lori and I just talked about Lori." It just popped out.

Neesha ducked her head. "Tanasha was into Tanasha too."

Joy reached for Neesha. She took hold of her hand and held it.

"Thanks for showin' me what to do when those boys in that car came by."

"That's all right. You caught on fast."

"And I'm really sorry about, you know, before too."

"Forget it. We worked it out. Made me think about Tanasha. She always had to be right. Even when she was wrong. *Especially* when she was wrong."

They started around the outside of the playground, more or less orbiting the courts where everybody else was playing basketball. They turned out to be pretty good skaters, so they raced a little just to see who was best. Then they played whip. Neesha reached back for Joy, then she returned the favor. Panting, they slumped on a splintery bench.

"So," asked Joy, "what's your school like?"

"It's okay."

"You guys wear uniforms and stuff?"

"Uh-uh. But my grandma thinks if everybody wore a school uniform and went to the bathroom first thing in the morning there'd be like no gangs and total world peace." She stood up and glided to a nearby fountain, took a long drink, then glided back. "Did your school have a metal detector?"

"The principal tried to talk about it once but everybody went ballistic."

"So there's not many guns?"

Joy shrugged. "There was one at school once, and it was in the town newspaper for about a month."

Neesha looked straight at her. "Are you going to go with me, or are you going to go to private school?"

"Depends on who you talk to—my mom or my dad."

"Come with me."

"I'll try."

Then they stood up and turned toward home. When Neesha waved to Cornell and his pals, Joy waved too. Cornell crowed, "See ya, wouldn't wanna be ya."

Neesha shook her head. "Daddy says everywhere he goes he sees boys balanced on the edge."

"What edge?"

"Well, like Cornell. He's pretty good in school, but his brother's in a gang. What's he going to do, you know? Which way's he gonna go?" Neesha shook her head. "My grandma prays for him every night."

Before Joy could say anything, somebody called, "Neesha!"

Way up the street, a woman waved.

"Who's that?" Joy asked.

"Mrs. Santiago. Come on. Let's say hi."

As they skated closer, Mrs. Santiago stepped into the middle of the sidewalk. She was dressed all in white: billowing skirt, long-sleeved blouse, scarf around her hair. Neesha skated right into her open arms, almost without slowing down. But Joy put on the brakes. She heard the lady ask, "Were those boys bothering you?"

Neesha shook her head. "It was just Cornell and his friends."

Mrs. Santiago motioned for Joy. "Come, child. There's room."

She just held out her hand. "I'm Joy Fontaine."

"I know. I spoke to Mrs. Park, who spoke to Neesha's grandmother. I have also been talking to Yemaya."

Joy edged closer. "Who's Yemaya?" She glanced at Neesha, but Mrs. Santiago answered, "You would call her a saint. She protects women in all their endeavors." She pointed to her yellow house. "Come inside. I have something for you."

The living room was crowded. A black man in a suit and tie paged through his newspaper; two Hispanic women held hands but argued softly in Spanish. A white lady, dressed all in yellow, looked like a worried banana.

Joy whispered to Neesha, "What is this, the rainbow room?"

"Shhh."

"Do all these people live here?"

"No."

Joy edged closer and whispered, "Something stinks."

"That's from the cigars. They're like part of her religion."

"So is this like a church—Our Lady of Second-hand Smoke?"

When the door opened and a man came in carrying a small cage, Joy asked, "What's he doing with that chicken?"

Neesha said, "It's for later, probably."

"For dinner?"

"Later than that."

"Oh, man. Tell me she hasn't got a doll with my name on it and a pin in its head."

On the table were candles, coconuts, a bowl of water, two oranges, some pennies, and a few pages of a newspaper called *Caribbean Sunrise*. Mrs. Santiago reached across all of that and offered Joy a narrow bracelet made from blue and yellow beads.

"Ochosi's colors. He has power over new houses."

Neesha whispered, "If you have any money, give her something and say, 'Thank you.'"

Joy dug in the pocket of her jeans, handed over a quarter, and thanked her.

Mrs. Santiago smiled and laid the money on a table beside three fat cigars. "Tell your father to come and see me, please."

Her voice was kind of tropical; each word seemed to take its time in her mouth. Not like Cornell's voice, which was edgy and raw; he pounded on some of the words like he was driving nails.

Then she shooed the girls back the way they'd come. When they went through the living room, everyone stood up in front of his or her straight-backed chair.

Outside, Joy looked at the bracelet, then at Neesha.

"Man, what was that?"

"Well, she helps people, you know?"

"Like a doctor?"

Neesha scratched her head. "Well, sort of. I've seen sick people go in her house. But she's like a psychologist too. One of the bus drivers my dad works with comes all the time. She has boyfriend problems."

"Does the bus driver get beads too?"

"Probably all the way up her arm. Debbie has lots of boyfriends."

Joy looked around. "This sure isn't like Wood-land Hills."

"AND THEN she said she wanted Dad to come see her." Joy put down her fork. "And look at this bracelet. It's from some saint who's into new houses."

Melissa frowned. "This Mrs. Santiago told you to tell your father to see her about some saint?"

"No. Just to talk, I think. It all happened pretty fast. She had patients waiting."

Melissa looked at Gregory, who helped himself to more salad.

"Patients?"

"Yeah. With love problems."

Joy's mother squared her shoulders. "So let me get this straight: a love doctor with coconuts in her living room wants to talk to your father."

"I don't think she's just a love doctor. One of the men in the waiting room had a chicken in a little cage."

"Oh, a combination love doctor and veterinarian. Then it's okay. Gregory, I definitely want you to go."

"She was really nice," Joy said.

Her father reached for the butter. "Look, I'll run into her on the street or in the market just like today when I ran into Mr. Ochoa, who owns the muffler shop. Then I'll see what's up."

Melissa's mother stabbed a piece of butter lettuce and looked at it. "If memory serves, there was very little voodoo in Woodland Hills."

"Oh," Joy said, "and that's not all that happened today. Neesha's teaching me stuff. Listen—'Few axe me, dat po dog be needin' hep.' " Then she got all her fingers right, waved her hands around, and bopped in the chair. "Know what I'm sayin'? Know what I'm sayin'?" Then she beamed at her parents.

Melissa stood up. She pointed her fork at Joy. "Young lady, I absolutely forbid you to talk like that!"

"But, Mom—"

"I mean it."

Gregory tugged at her wrist. "Oh, Melissa, relax."

"You relax. You're not the one sending out cops and EMTs to pick up some kid who's yelling, 'I be shot! I be shot!' "

Gregory turned his coffee cup one way, then another. Joy fiddled with her broccoli.

Her mom put one hand to her forehead, as if she were taking her own temperature. "I'm sorry." She looked at Joy. "But I can't stand that kind of talk."

Joy looked down at her plate. "Yes, ma'am."

Her mother pushed back her chair again, just not so forcefully this time. "I'm going to go upstairs and lie down for about a year."

Gregory just nodded. Joy brushed some crumbs off the table and caught them in her hand. By the time she'd walked to the sink, her mother was out of earshot. She turned to her father.

"Neesha doesn't have to talk like that. She just knows how."

"I know, sweetie. Your mom does too." He motioned for her. Joy slumped on his lap, her forehead against his.

"I guess we're not going to play It Never Happened?"

"Not right now."

"Is she going to make us move?"

"Don't tell me you're starting to like it here."

"Well, maybe. A little."

4

Neesha and Joy drank milk. Gregory sat at the kitchen table too, a slender number 4 sable paintbrush clenched between his teeth.

"You look like a pirate," said Neesha. "In this video I saw they carried their knives that way."

"I uz ooing is unce—"

"Speak English, Dad."

He removed the paintbrush and said, "I was doing this once when I had a terrific idea. I was sort of hoping if I did it again I'd have another one." He rubbed his jaw. "Instead I kind of gave myself a toothache."

"So paint a picture of a dentist," suggested Neesha.

Melissa came downstairs, her brown clogs thunking on every step. "What's so funny?" She reached into the refrigerator.

"You had to be there," said her husband.

Melissa circled the table. She kissed all three of them good-bye. "I don't want anything bad to happen," she said, "but yesterday I got way too many calls asking how to find Disneyland. Now who would dial 911 for that?"

"Some guy from Minnesota," said Gregory, "who's been driving in a circle on these free-ways."

"With a backseat full of kids."

"Kids with diarrhea," said Neesha, and she and Joy giggled.

"You've got a point."

Neesha tugged at her SEA WORLD T-shirt. "Mrs. Fontaine, is it fun to work at the 911 center, or is it sad?"

"It's mostly nerve-racking. But it's funny some-times."

"Like when?"

"Lizard Lips," Joy said, and her mom smiled.

Neesha wanted to know who Lizard Lips was.

"One of the firefighters. He got talked into giv-ing this iguana mouth-to-mouth."

Neesha made a face. "Yuk."

"The first time, it was a real call. There really was a fire, and the iguana really did sort of pass out from the smoke, and the firefighter just did it to quiet the woman down. But now she calls up all the time: the iguana's having a heart attack, the iguana's in respiratory arrest, the iguana's lonely."

"And the fat guy in the bathtub?" said Gregory.

"Oh yeah. Calls from his cell phone. He's stuck and can't get out. So I dispatch a unit. They have to break down the door. And there's this guy who looks like Moby Dick. He's crying and eating a half gallon of ice cream. The firefighter wants to know if he's so stuck, how'd he get the mocha fudge. He says that he brought it in there with him."

"So how'd they get him out?"

"It took a whole can of Crisco, but he finally popped out."

When she stopped laughing, Neesha said, "These are as good as my dad's bus driver stories."

Then Melissa kissed them all good-bye again, and Joy made toast for three.

A few minutes later, Neesha asked, "What time is your friend coming?"

"Pretty soon. Her mom's going to call from the car, so we can meet her outside. Right, Dad?"

Gregory stuck his napkin in his book. "I hope. I had my map, she had her map, but she kept saying, 'Are you sure?' "

"Lori's mom's a scaredy-cat. She was always the first one outside school, like at two-thirty."

Gregory waved his book and looked around. "Did you know that all this used to be a ranch?"

"The kitchen? Pretty small ranch, Dad."

"El Rancho Mesa." Neesha tapped the table.

"Girls, girls." Gregory waved both hands. "No more sugar this morning."

"Sorry. We're dying to hear about local history. Aren't we dying, Neesha?"

"I'm not dying, but I don't feel so good."

He held up the book. "I like knowing there's been cattle here and cowboys and then muddy streets and then train tracks and then concrete, 'cause whatever was here is still here. Maybe you can't see it, but it's not gone." He turned over his book. "Hmmmm." Then he stood up, paused for a minute, and wandered away.

"Where's he going?" asked Neesha.

"Whenever he starts that 'Hmmmm' stuff it means he's going to his studio."

"I think I want to be an artist too."

"I think I want to be a bus driver." Joy pretended that she was holding a big steering wheel.

Neesha shook her head. "Nah, Dad'd just tell you the same thing he told me: 'Honey, you can do better than that.'"

"Well, I can't be an artist 'cause I can't draw."

"Just drip. Your dad's got that one picture that's all drips, right?"

"I think it's harder than it looks."

"Drippin' is hard? What's hard about it?"

"Well, you have to kind of decide where to drip, I think."

"So? Decide."

"I don't know, Neesha."

"I'd help you."

"Artists don't work together. They're always off by themselves and stuff."

"Then we'll be the first."

"Your grandma told Mom that you wanted to be a lawyer."

Neesha's glass left a wet circle on the white tabletop. She moved it and started to play with the water. She turned the circle into a beak, turned that into a triangle.

"Grandma wants me to want to be a lawyer. That's different from me wantin' to be one. 'Nother thing she's always tellin' me is, 'Girl, you go out in that big white world, but don't forget you were born right here on Ibarra Street.' " Neesha made a face. "Sounds like a Whitney Houston movie." She stared up toward the ceiling. "I think your dad's got it made. He just reads and thinks and then drips and makes money."

Just then the phone rang. Joy reached for it, said hello, listened. She motioned for Neesha. "It's Lori!"

Joy looped one arm around Neesha's shoulders and held the receiver between them so they could both hear.

"Bring a hat," Joy said.

"Bring your skates," said Neesha.

"Hold on. I'll call him." Joy reached for the intercom buttons beside the wall phone. "Dad, talk to Lori's mom, please."

The girls leaned against the wall. Joy held the phone so she and Neesha could eavesdrop.

"Mrs. Garland," said Gregory, "it's perfectly safe. We've lived here two whole weeks and nothing's happened. The streets are full of people. There are as many police cars as in Woodland Hills, I can guarantee that. There are lots of safe streets, and I gave you the safest route. Yes, and I'll be outside waiting. I'll be wearing a suit of armor. That was a joke. Yes, good-bye."

Joy put back the receiver. "Lori's mom's just a little weird." She looked around. "Let's clean up the kitchen before they get here."

They worked side by side. Joy wiped down the blue tile counter and oak table; Neesha washed and dried dishes. Joy put away things, then she sponged off the chrome stove and Neesha swept the hardwood floor.

But instead of using a dustpan or a vacuum cleaner, she opened the back door and swept the few crumbs out onto the old concrete steps and then into the raggedy lawn so the birds could have them.

Neesha sat down on the steps. She ran her hand over the chipped concrete. She looked down at the layers of colors.

"Man, think of all the different people who painted these old steps. They probably moved in and wanted the place to look nice, just like you guys did." She pried at a loose chip, streaked like a rainbow. "I bet there was another girl that sat right here."

Joy settled beside her. The back of a big, old warehouse made a wall where the property ended. Growing halfway up that were sunflowers. Their faces were turned up, like people looking for UFOs.

"Who planted those, I wonder?"

"Not those homeless creeps last year, that's for sure."

"Yeah, I remember. One of your dad's friends said he had to call the police."

Neesha nodded. *"Everybody* called the police. It was so bad. Grandma was praying all the time."

Joy glanced at her Wonder Woman watch. "We better go out front and wait."

Neesha brushed at the seat of her purple shorts. "It's sure better to leave nice things like sunflowers instead of crack vials."

Joy stopped. "People used drugs in here?"

"They started to. Scared everybody to death. That stuff belongs on Nasty Street."

Joy touched the intercom button. "Dad, we're going out to wait for Lori. Are you coming?"

"Be right there."

They drifted outside, pulling the door shut tight behind them. It was hot and still. The sky looked like good silverware that'd been kept in a bottom drawer too long. That tarnished color.

"Maybe," said Neesha, "we should just go to the beach and skate. The nine hundred bus'll get us there in about half an hour."

"I've never been on a regular bus, just a school bus."

Just then a sharky-looking Chevrolet with tinted windows cruised around the corner. The girls could hear the pounding bass.

"I think some guy in that car almost spit at me," Joy whispered, "the day after we moved in here."

"Lucky it didn't hit you. Probably would've eaten right through your sandals. That's some of The Condemned."

"A real gang?"

"Uh-huh. If they go by, don't stare at them or say anything."

"Don't worry."

"They're going," Neesha reported. "They're going the other way now." Then she waved.

"I thought you said not to do anything."

Neesha pointed. "I'm waving to him."

Across the street was the homeless man Joy had seen on her way to Ibarra Street that first time. He still had a train of grocery carts. They still looked full of what her mother had called broken glass and toxic waste.

"You know that guy?" Joy asked.

"Oh yeah. For years. He's cool."

"Not one of the creeps who lived in our house and smoked crack?"

"No way." Neesha waved again, and he started to haul his carts across the almost empty intersection.

Just then Gregory walked up behind them. "What a coincidence. A minute ago I was just looking at some Polaroids, and there he was."

"His name's Dimitrios," said Neesha.

"Is he okay?" asked Joy.

Neesha nodded her head. "Dimitrios wouldn't hurt anybody."

Dimitrios dragged his carts toward them and lined them up at the curb. Sweating, he wiped his face with a dazzling white handkerchief as he approached. Joy took in his red pants, sandals with tire soles, yellow shirt. His hat was soft and colored red, black, and green. Dreadlocks hung over his creased face.

"I was looking forward to seeing you today," he said. "You've been in all my dreams."

"You've been dreaming about us?" asked Joy.

"I saw us talking. I'm so pleased that it came true." He put one arm around Neesha. "Have you been well, child?"

"You used to dream about me," she said, grinning. "Grandma would say that's just like a man."

"I don't suppose," asked Gregory, "that there's a packed gallery in these dreams? With people bidding furiously on my new work?"

Dimitrios frowned. He closed his eyes. "There was no gallery, and you weren't the artist, but there was new work."

Suddenly Joy pointed. "Look! Here comes Lori!"

A big silver Mercedes angled toward them, then pulled up in front of the house. Joy grinned at Lori as the electric window slid down.

"Hi!" Joy tried the door, but it was locked. "I hope you remembered your skates. This is Neesha."

Lori poked one arm out and shook hands with Neesha, but she kept her eyes on Dimitrios. "We, uh, can't stay as long as I said. Exactly. My tennis lesson's been changed."

"You're kidding."

"No, it's at one-thirty now, so . . ." Her voice faded away.

Joy stepped back. She felt Neesha's warm arm against hers. "Well, at least see the house, okay? And we've got lunch and stuff."

"It looks very nice, Joy. But my lesson's been changed."

"You already said that." Joy looked at her

father, then back at her friend, who was inspecting her strawberry-colored hair. "You aren't even going to stay for a minute, are you? You're going home now."

Lori looked at her mother. "Well, we could stay for a minute, I guess."

That's when Dimitrios's carts started rolling. The third one—with the horse's tail and the reflectors—swung slowly and bounced off the Mercedes.

"Oh, my God!" Lori's mother clutched her pearls; the other hand gripped the pearl-colored steering wheel. "What did I tell you! It's a bump-and-run car-jacking; I read about it in *Newsweek*. Get away from the window, sweetheart! Back in the car. Back."

She reached for Lori, slammed the car into reverse, powered up over the curb with a squeal and a thunk, gunned it, and went zooming back the way she'd come.

Everybody just stared after her. Nobody said a word until Joy blurted, "No way is she my friend anymore."

Neesha looked down the street. "The old grocery cart car-jacking scam? What *Newsweek*'s she been reading."

"I never liked that woman," said Gregory. His arm slipped around Joy's shoulders.

Dimitrios stepped forward and asked, "Would

it be all right with you if I buy the girls a soft drink?"

"Up to them."

"I'm in," said Neesha.

"Why not," said Joy. "I'm not going skating with my dear friend Lori." She shook her head in disgust.

"Maybe," said Gregory, "I'll just tag along."

"You should go see Mrs. Santiago," Dimitrios said. "Let her throw the shells."

Gregory hesitated. He looked down at his daughter.

"I'm okay, Dad."

"Really?"

"Really. I was tired of Lori and her stupid classes, anyway."

"So I guess I'll go see Mrs. Santiago, throw a shell or two." He grinned at Joy and Neesha. "I didn't want things to be like they were in Woodland Hills, did I? I wanted new experiences. This'll be a new experience, right?"

Dimitrios checked his carts one more time, tucking them into the curb and—this time—blocking the wheels. Then he and Neesha and Joy walked to Park's Market. They were just inside the door when Mr. Park reached for a broom.

"Want to sweep, Dimitrios?" he asked. "Work off what you owe?"

"In a bit, perhaps." He looked down at the girls and smiled. He leaned forward. His breath smelled like cloves. "Get whatever you want."

Neesha and Joy drifted toward the back of the store. They stood in front of the lighted cooler. "You really okay?" asked Neesha.

"Uh-huh."

"Maybe her mom scared her to death on the way down here. Grown-ups'll do that."

Joy looked at the bottles of soda: the colas, the orange, the strawberry, the 7UP. All standing together. "Yeah," she said finally. "Maybe."

When the girls put their drinks on the counter Dimitrios said, "This is my treat." He gave Mr. Park two carefully folded bills. "This is to help make up for frightening your friend away, Joy. If it hadn't been for me, she might have stayed."

"Once," Joy said. "Big deal."

They walked out into the sunlight, squinting. Dimitrios took a bottle of water from the woven bag he carried over one shoulder. "Shall we sit down?"

Neesha and Joy looked at each other. "On the sidewalk?"

Dimitrios didn't just plop down, he descended. "Before the market was here, a long time ago," he said, "there was a church. People sat in rows and sang and prayed and got married and buried each other. So this is a good place."

The girls shrugged and settled beside him. Then all looked out at the busy street.

"You know," said Joy, "she really wasn't my only friend. I had a couple of others. So I was thinking I should call up Amber and Corrina. Get their moms to bring them down. Maybe this time Mrs. Santiago'll be out in the middle of the street waving a chicken around. We could bet on whether the Lexus or the Jaguar would get to the freeway first."

Neesha grinned. "Tell it, girl. Make their ears burn."

Joy took a long drink. "She was just so rude."

"Forget it," advised Neesha. "You've got plenty of friends."

"Plenty? You're the only friend I've got!"

"No way. What about my dad and my grandma? What about Mrs. Santiago and Mr. Lossi? Everybody on Ibarra Street's your friend."

"It's true," said Dimitrios. "Everywhere I go people say what a nice young lady you are. They call you a ray of pure sunlight."

"Really?"

Across the street, Cornell shot by on his bike. He glanced their way, then pedaled faster.

Dimitrios looked at Neesha. "I think Cornell likes you."

"Time before last I saw him, he threw half an old taco at me. Did Romeo throw Mexican food at Juliet?"

Dimitrios turned to Joy. "Do you have a suitor too?"

"Bobby Collins put a note in my locker once with these little boxes that said check here if you love me, or check here if you like me. Except he spelled *here h-e-a-r*."

"Check here if you need tutoring," said Neesha.

Joy raised the Pepsi to her lips, then hesitated. "Would you like some, Dimitrios?"

"No, thank you," he said. "This is the time of year to drink pure water and to eat yellow vegetables."

"No pizza?"

He shook his head. "I eat what's abundant and inexpensive."

"Where do you live?"

"Everywhere."

"What's the zip code for that, all zeros?"

Dimitrios laughed, showing his white teeth. "No one writes to me. I get no bills, pay no taxes."

Just then Mr. Park came to the front door. "Dimitrios! Work, please. Now."

"No, thank you."

Mr. Park muttered in Korean and turned away.

Dimitrios closed his eyes. "Everywhere people say, 'Follow your dream.' So I do, and they're upset with me."

Neesha leaned toward him. "I hate to be the one to break this to you, D., but they don't mean like nighttime dreams; they mean goals and stuff."

"Do you do what your dreams tell you?" asked Joy.

"I do what I do and watch what happens."

"Are your dreams always right?"

"Oh, no. Merely true."

Joy leaned forward and looked at Neesha, who shrugged and rolled her eyes.

Joy looked at the entrance to the market. "If you don't dream about work, how do you buy things?"

"The government sends a check to the pastor of Neesha's church. Then he gives me what I need."

"Couldn't you save up and rent an apartment?"

"Walls keep my dreams in."

"Aren't you lonely?"

"No."

"Do you get scared?"

"Sometimes. There are bad people on the streets. Desperate people."

"Have you got a gun or a stick or something in your carts?"

"No. When I have dreams of danger, I'm very, very careful."

When Neesha nudged her, Joy said, "Too many questions?"

"No." She held out a Dr Pepper. "Want to trade?"

They swapped bottles. Each took a long drink, then they both burped at exactly the same time.

When Joy stopped giggling she asked Dimitrios, "Where do you sleep?"

"In bad weather, I go to the shelter, but I don't like it there. It's noisy and the people are crude." He pointed across the street and down a little. "I used to like to unroll my sleeping bag by the side of that little white house. There's a tree there that I like and that likes me." Dimitrios drank water out of a plastic bottle. "Since the Castillo family moved out, I can't sleep there anymore. I have an uneasy feeling about the place."

"Where did the Castillos go?" asked Neesha.

"Back to Mexico, I imagine."

Joy squinted. The house was white with one concrete step. It didn't sit square on its foundation. It seemed to have bad posture.

"Won't somebody else just move in?" she asked.

Dimitrios nodded and rubbed his calloused hands together. "Probably, but who? Every time I go over there, I'm cold."

"So?" asked Neesha.

"It isn't cold out. I've never been cold there before. So I'm afraid it's going to be unlucky again."

Then he looked at Joy. "Your house, on the

other hand, is very lucky. Now it's happier than it's been for a long time."

Neesha nudged Joy. "Here comes your dad."

Gregory made his way toward them. When he was close enough, Joy asked, "What happened?"

"Well," he said, scratching his head, "she was very nice. She said how glad she was that we'd moved down here, and if I wanted to sell a lot of paintings I should wrap some canvas around a potato, sprinkle it with chicken's blood, and bury it at midnight."

Joy scrambled to her feet. "Are you gonna?"

"Well, I might, but I'm fresh out of chicken's blood."

"I believe," said Dimitrios, "beet juice would do."

"So I wrap some canvas around a potato, squeeze a beet, and bury *that* at midnight?"

"Yes."

"I couldn't do this while my wife's at work, could I?"

Dimitrios shrugged. "Noon isn't the same as midnight."

"You know, I don't really believe it's going to help me paint better."

"Perhaps Mrs. Santiago believes enough for both of you."

"Well, okay, I guess." He glanced at the girls. "But . . ."

Neesha and Joy said it together: "Don't tell your mother."

They laughed, then Gregory laughed, then Dimitrios joined in. All of them standing in front of Park's Market in the late morning sun, laughing.

July

5

EVERYBODY WAS SITTING on Neesha's front porch, and everybody means Joy and her parents, Neesha and her dad and grandma. From the muffler shop came the sound of Mr. Ochoa pounding.

Joy leaned back against her dad's legs and took a deep breath. She loved sitting on the porch. When they lived in the loft downtown, there was just the fire escape, and you couldn't sit out there. There were porches in Woodland Hills, but nobody ever used them. On Ibarra Street, everybody sat out.

"Let's go down to the gate," Joy said.

Neesha reached for the cookies. "We'd better take some provisions. It's a rigorous journey."

She was wearing skates; Joy was barefoot and

careful to keep her toes out of the way. The palm trees that lined Ibarra Street leaned to the east a little. In the dusk, the top of each one looked like a little explosion.

Half a block or so away, the owner came out of his shoe repair shop. He was just reaching for the big metal gate that pulled down and kept his store safe when he spotted Joy and Neesha. Then he walked toward them a dozen yards or so, stopped, and shouted, *"Joy, tu padre quiere sus zapatos?"*

"Something about my dad's shoes."

"Yeah, does he want them."

Joy turned. "Dad? Do you want your shoes? Enrique's closing up."

"Tomorrow is fine."

Joy waved back. *"Mañana!* Okay?"

The girls watched him get on his bike and wave to Mr. Lossi, who glided past in his car.

The spotless Oldsmobile pulled up in front of Neesha's house. Mr. Lossi got out and opened the door for Miriam, who ran the beauty shop down the street. She smiled down at the girls, leaned over the gate, and asked, "Melissa! Are you comin' in Saturday?"

"Yes. And Joy too."

Miriam had long fingernails. Very long and very curved. She ran them through Joy's curls. "Child, this could be angel hair; instead it looks like it come out of a mattress."

Mr. Lossi handed over a bag of groceries. "I can drive you the rest of the way home, Miriam," he said. "I'd be glad to."

"No, no." She pounded on her hips with one hand. "I need the exercise. Thanks for carryin' me this far."

"Do you want to come up and sit down, Mr. Lossi?" asked Neesha politely.

He shook his head. "No, thank you. I just want to ask everybody one question."

So the girls followed him up the walk, where he took off his black hat and shook everyone's hand.

"I was just thinking," he said, "of buying tickets to a Dodger game. Like last year. Miriam's coming, and Mr. Ochoa."

Neesha's dad shifted his chair toward the screen door so his mother, who'd gone inside, could hear. "Do you want to go to a baseball game, Momma?"

"Absolutely!"

Neesha nudged Joy. "Baseball is great," she whispered. "I eat until I almost throw up, and then I lean on my dad and go to sleep."

"Can we go too, Dad?" asked Joy.

"Why not? Right, Mel?"

Neesha whispered, "Last year Mrs. Santiago put, like, this temporary curse on the other team."

Joy whispered back, "Mrs. Santiago goes to baseball games?"

"Everybody goes to baseball games."

"I've seen them on television."

"You've never been to Dodger Stadium?"

"Uh-uh."

Neesha shook her head and pretended to be solemn. "Another deprived child in the midst of plenty. Film at eleven."

Everybody said good-bye to Mr. Lossi, and they settled on the porch again. Joy leaned against her father's legs. She heard someone pour lemonade. Mrs. Kincaid's voice filtered out through the screen door. She could feel her dad idly sketching something on a piece of folded-up paper.

"How's your painting going, Greg?" asked Walter.

Gregory shrugged. "Up until yesterday it was going great. Today I've got nothing but problems."

"Maybe," said Joy, "you should've used a bigger potato."

Her father scowled at her. "Shhh."

"Or a bigger beet."

"Shhhhhh!"

Neesha glided over. She picked up Gregory's hand and put her small fingertips on his larger ones. She patted his arm. "You should skate more. Whenever I have a problem, I go out and skate, and by the time I get back home I know what to do."

Gregory laughed and put one arm around her. "You are the sweetest child in the world."

Joy tugged at her mom's denim shirt. "Do you have a piece of paper? I want to write that down so when I go on *Oprah* and cry I'll have it right."

"You're the sweetest, then. Actually, you're both the sweetest. It's a tie."

"That's pitiful, Dad."

"What you should do, Greg," said Walter, "is join my gym. It sounds to me like you're cooped up too many hours of the day."

"You're probably right, but I'm doing good work. I showed some to Josh, my agent, and he got pretty excited." He took a deep breath. "I was right about Ibarra Street."

"I'm glad we moved," said Joy.

Melissa raised her glass of lemonade. Just then, a big black car turned onto Ibarra Street. With its tinted windows it seemed like part of the night had broken off and was drifting through the streets.

Walter sat up straight. "Bad news."

"What?"

"That bunch is from Nasty Street again. I don't like this."

Melissa motioned for Joy to come closer. "What bunch is that?" she asked.

"They're drug dealers. Serious, full-time criminals. Somebody in the market told me they've been cruising by all week."

Everybody watched the car stop in front of the Castillo house, the one that Dimitrios used to sleep beside, the one that had been empty for weeks now.

The car doors swung open and three young guys got out.

Two of them were skinny, and their huge clothes hung all over them. The other one was fat, and his T-shirt and pants were way too tight. It looked like they'd been shopping at the wrong stores.

They stood on the sidewalk and looked the place over. Everyone else looked them over: the Parks came out of their store, Mr. Lossi leaned across the hood of his car, Mrs. Santiago stood in her front door. Up and down the street, porches and windows filled with people.

"Maybe I should go talk to them," Gregory said.

Neesha's father wrapped a big hand around his wrist. "What are you gonna do, shake your paintbrush at them?"

"I'd just explain the situation: this is mostly a residential street, there are lots of families and kids, it's a busy thoroughfare—"

"Gregory, you're so green, if I planted you, you'd grow."

"What? Why?"

"The Parks tried to 'explain the situation' to those men once."

"I bet I know what happened." Melissa fell back in her chair. "But tell me, anyway."

"They were just taking anything they wanted off the shelves," said Neesha. "I saw 'em."

Walter reached for his daughter. "So the Parks told them to stop or they'd call the police. They just got laughed at. So they call the police, but by the time they get there, the bad guys are gone.

"Then that night somebody drives by and breaks all the windows in the store. Now they just take what they want."

"Why are they looking at that little house?" asked Joy.

"Probably because they want to sell drugs from there."

She frowned. "Let's call the police."

Walter shook his head. "Right now they're not doing anything against the law. We hassle them tonight, six hours from now they break our windows."

"They wouldn't know it was us," said Neesha.

"They'd just break *all* the windows on this part of Ibarra Street. Everybody's."

Just then, Mrs. Kincaid came out of the house.

"Mr. Green's poorly again," she muttered. Then she asked, "What's happened? What's everybody looking at?"

Her son pointed. "Looks like those hard cores over there are thinking about going into business on Ibarra Street."

She nudged her red, plastic visor, then reached to steady her glasses. She leaned forward and squinted. "I know that child."

"You might have known him once, Momma, but he's not what he was then, and he surely is not a child."

"Well, he is to me. I've seen him in a diaper."

Before anybody could say or do anything, she was down the walk.

"Grandma!"

Walter pushed Neesha against Gregory, who held on; then he ran down the walk. Too late. His mother had charged between cars and was already across the street.

"Grandma!"

Everybody on the street moved closer. They filtered out of their houses, or down their sidewalks, or onto the curb as Mrs. Kincaid backed the three young men up just by shaking her finger at them. She pointed to the shabby house with one of her big red fingernails. She pointed at their car.

She seemed to be doing fine. She seemed to be backing them right off of Ibarra Street when all of a sudden one of them pushed back. Pushed hard, and down she went.

The whole street gasped as the gangstas turned, strutted to their car, and sped away.

6

THE NEXT EVENING, everybody met in front of Park's Market. Neesha and Joy slipped in and out of the crowd of neighbors, who milled around and muttered.

Neesha's father stood up on a bench. He wore serious clothes: polished shoes, gray slacks, a white shirt and tie.

"The kind of people we're talking about here," he said, "will come into a neighborhood with the intention of selling drugs out of an abandoned house and then knock down an elderly person in the bargain. And we all know that's just the beginning because they're capable of a lot worse than that."

"I get a gun!" That was Mr. Park. "I get a gun and shoot them."

Someone yelled from the back, "I know what I'm gonna do. I'm gettin' my family out of here any way I can."

Mr. Lossi made his way through the muttering and the nodding. He was dressed up too. Besides the black suit, he wore a diamond pin in his tie and a black snap-brim hat. He stood beside Walter on the bench. When he raised one hand for silence, his sleeve slid back to reveal a gold watch.

"Let me handle this," he rasped. "I'll make a few calls and—"

Mr. Park hooted at him. "You said that when same men stole food from me. 'Let me handle it, I take care of it.' Then nothing happened. They took what they wanted, then broke windows. Maybe you powerful man one day, but no more." He pounded himself on the chest. "I buy a gun."

Joy leaned over and asked Neesha if it was true that Mr. Lossi had been a powerful man once.

"Dad says so. But it was a long time ago."

Gregory took Mr. Lossi's place on the bench. In his shorts and T-shirt, he looked like he'd just come from the beach.

"Wouldn't everything be all right if somebody lived in that house? Why can't we just get a relative or a friend to move in?"

"What you mean," said Mr. Jardin, the sharp-looking man who'd been playing cards on Neesha's porch, "is one of *our* friends. Somebody black who don't matter much in case The Condemned come down on them."

"That isn't what I meant at all. I meant—"

"All right then, all right then. Put your white money where your white mouth is and get one of your friends to sign a long-term lease."

"Having somebody move in there is a good idea," said Walter. "But it's not just up to Greg here."

When Mrs. Santiago raised her hand and started for the bench, Neesha nudged Joy. "C'mon."

"Where?"

"Let's go look at the house. All they're going to do is talk and talk and talk. Mrs. Santiago is going to say she spoke to one of her saints. Then Grandma is going to show everybody her bruise and say we should all pray. Then Mr. Park is—"

"Going to want a gun."

"You got that right. Your dad had the best idea so far, except Mr. Jardin won't listen to anything a white man says. But every time he gets married, he marries a lighter-skinned lady. So go figure."

"You know what else is weird about him? His name is French, just like ours. *Jardin* means 'garden,' like *Fontaine* means 'fountain.' Doesn't he get it, that we're at least a little bit like each other?"

Half a block away, beside the muffler shop, stood *the* house—a little old stucco with a slanty porch. Two windows flanked a door with the paint peeling off.

"They're like sick people," Joy said, looking at the dried-up lawn, "with nobody to take care of them. So they just get worse."

Joy laid one hand on her friend's shoulder, and they both peered at the house for a long minute.

"I wonder if this looks like a crack house already," Joy asked, "or do they do something to it?"

Neesha shook her head. "Dunno."

"People smoke crack, right?"

"Uh-huh. And then they fall down."

"That sounds so stupid."

"And then I guess you want more. And after a while you don't want anything else."

Joy stepped off the sidewalk and knelt down on the so-called lawn. She put her hand flat on the dirt, like she was taking its temperature.

"What if we did what your grandma does," she said. "But we'd do it to the house."

"Bring it some soup?"

"Sort of. We could sweep up and water the lawn, anyway."

Neesha gave Joy a hand up. "It couldn't hurt, could it?"

7

THE NEXT DAY was a Saturday, and they spent most of the morning at the house. Joy found a hose out back and watered the tree, the scrawny bushes, and the lawn while Neesha swept the steps and walk. When a car backfired, Joy said, "Wave to Mom so she'll know we're all right."

While they were working, Mrs. Santiago came across the street. She was all in white, as usual, except for a gingham apron. She had her hand in the apron pocket, rattling something.

When she got right up to them, she held out three stones.

"Each of these stands for one of the men who knocked Mrs. Kincaid down." She tossed them on the ground. "Kick them around. Stand on them. That way you dominate the person, and you will have nothing to fear."

The girls looked down at the stones.

"I'd rather throw them at their big dumb heads."

Mrs. Santiago chuckled. "Just humiliate the stones. The men will not come back." Then she crossed the street to her yellow house.

Pretty soon Mr. Lossi started toward them.

"Under the circumstances, maybe you girls should play somewhere closer to home."

"We're not playing, we're—"

"But if anything should happen"—he held up a black cellular phone—"I make one call."

"To the police?" asked Neesha.

"Better than the police," he said. He patted their heads. "I've got my eye on you, but don't be too long, all right?"

When he was out of earshot, Neesha said, "I hate it when people pat me on the head. I'm not a cocker spaniel."

"Maybe," said Joy, "you ought to stop carrying that old tennis ball around in your mouth."

Neesha wiped at her forehead. "I'm hot."

"Me too." Joy twisted the nozzle on the hose until the water stopped. "Maybe we're done, anyhow. I mean, it probably looks as good as we're gonna get it."

The way the tires yelped made them both jump. Dimitrios tugged his carts across the street as drivers yelled at him. It took at least a minute for him to get to them.

"What are you two up to today?" he asked.

Neesha smiled. "We thought maybe if we fixed this place up a little, it wouldn't turn into a crack house."

Dimitrios wiped his streaming face with a clean handkerchief. "Well, it's already a cracked house."

"What?"

"Look. From the earthquake. There's a little crack running from up there by the roof all across the front."

"I don't think that's gonna stop The Condemned," said Neesha.

"What a stupid name." Joy dropped the hose into the dust. "Why'd they call themselves that?"

"A very interesting question," said Dimitrios. "Is a name part of your destiny? Are The Condemned the way they are just because of their name? Or do they make it come true?"

Joy frowned as Neesha yelled, "Dimitrios, can I have some of your broken mirrors?"

"I've been saving them for you."

Neesha ran toward him. "Really?"

"I dreamed I picked them up. I dreamed that I saved them. I just didn't dream who they were for."

Neesha tugged at his sleeve. "And is that gunk in the other cart like glue or something?"

"For you, also."

"Sup, due?" Joy asked, and Neesha grinned.

"I was thinking—what if we stuck mirrors to the house."

"Yeah. And?"

"And when people came to buy drugs they'd have to look at themselves."

"So?"

"So, they're not gonna look good, right? And maybe they change their minds or something. Decide to buy a new shirt instead or call their mom or something."

"Yeah!" said Joy. "So then the drug sellers would go out of business!"

Both of them looked at Dimitrios. "What do you think?"

"It's a wonderful idea, and your parents will hate it."

"Why?"

"To begin with—the broken glass."

"Oh yeah. All they're going to say is, 'You could put your eye out.' Why do grown-ups think we're always gonna poke our eyes out?"

"But I have plastic goggles," said Dimitrios. "For protection."

"Really?"

"Yes, and gloves."

"Cool. Let's get started!"

The goggles were fine, but the gloves were another story. One was an oven mitten, one was a red leather dress glove, one was the stripey kind with a cuff that a railroad man might wear, and the fourth was brown cotton. It had been run over. A lot.

"Now don't argue over the stylish red glove," Dimitrios cautioned. "I know how pretty young ladies are."

Joy asked, "How do you know how pretty young ladies are?"

"Oh, from another life."

Neesha looked at Joy. Joy looked at Neesha. "Right," they said.

Dimitrios unloaded two heavy boxes, both full of mirrors. Then from the third cart he hauled out a big plastic drum of glue with the label nearly ripped off.

Joy wore the railroad man's glove and the trashed brown one. Neesha put her left hand in the oven mitten, her right in the red glove, which fit her perfectly.

"So," she said, rubbing her palms together. "Let's go to work."

It went pretty fast because they made a little assembly line: Joy got to plunge her hand deep into the sticky glue, then dab some on the backs of the broken mirrors and pass them along.

Neesha started to outline the door of the house. She stood on a box and reached as high as she could; then Dimitrios took over while she pointed. Every little bit, she stopped, ran up the walk a ways, cocked her head, and looked at what they were doing.

Later, while Dimitrios and Joy were waiting for Neesha to decide which of the last pieces to put where, Joy said, "When Dad was in advertising, he said they didn't use milk in ads for cereal. They used Elmer's Glue because it was whiter."

"My father was Greek; instead of cereal, we ate mountains of couscous."

"Is your father alive?"

He shook his head. "And my mother went back to Cuba when she got sick."

"Gee, you're all alone."

"Oh, no." He smiled down at her. "Not at all."

Neesha strolled back to them. "It's okay, but it needs something."

"Like what?" Joy asked, looking at the upside-down horseshoe of glass over the door.

Neesha narrowed her eyes. "Look who's coming."

Joy turned around. "So much for the Mrs. Santiago theory of crime prevention."

That long, sharky car zipped up to the curb, and three young men scrambled out. Dimitrios stepped in front of the girls. The biggest hoodlum grabbed him by his yellow T-shirt.

"Whaddya think you're doin', old man?" He was the strongest of them all; he wore a stocking cap, and his big head seemed to sit right on his shoulders without bothering with a neck.

Dimitrios just hung in the man's hands. When he was dropped to the ground, he collapsed like a Slinky. Pulled up, he rose smoothly as smoke.

The other two men shoved out their chests, bumping him. They both made their fingers into birds' beaks and pecked at Dimitrios.

"Stay away from here, you know what I'm sayin'? Just stay away."

Neesha took a step forward. "*You* stay away. You don't live here, and nobody wants you to."

He dropped Dimitrios again, then shook a very large finger at her. His OAKLAND RAIDERS T-shirt shimmered. "And you shut up!"

Joy stepped up beside her friend. "Don't tell her to shut up. You shut up, you po dog. You don't, you be needin' hep put yo pants on."

The leader looked at his buddies; then he laughed, showing a lot of gold teeth; then he loomed over her.

"Listen, Snowball. You way outta your depth here, you know what I'm sayin'? Way out. Now you git while I impress this old man here with the seriousness of the situation."

Joy started to yell, "Mr. Lossi! Mr. Lossi!"

Neesha backed away too. "Dad! Grandma!"

"People comin'," said one of the men.

The leader shook Dimitrios one more time. "This gonna be our house, you know what I'm sayin'? So just stay away from here. Don't make me hurt you now." Then he threw him on the sidewalk and followed the other two to the car, which slithered up to meet them.

The girls ran to Dimitrios. Everyone else ran to them.

Melissa pulled Joy to her. "What did they want?"

"They want us to stop working on the house," said Neesha.

Joy pointed. "We were fixing it up."

"Well, I'm calling the police," Melissa said.

Mr. Lossi held up his portable phone. "Already done. The minute they pulled up."

Mrs. Park lectured Dimitrios, who was sitting comfortably on the ground. "You mess around, make things worse. Stop it. You can go any-where. Not us."

Neesha's father knelt down. "You okay, honey?"

"Sure. They just yelled at us."

Gregory ran one hand through his daughter's long, fair hair. Then he looked around. "What are the mirrors around the front door for?"

"So the people who want to buy drugs would have to see themselves first."

Gregory nodded. "Interesting."

Melissa shook her head. "Oh, no. I know what that means. I've heard 'interesting' before. This isn't interesting; this is dangerous. This is not art; it's life."

"But it *is* art," said Gregory. "That's the point." He looked at the girls. "Is it done?"

Neesha shook her head. "It needs something."

Joy blurted, "I know. It needs a big crack down the front of the house." She pointed. "Right where the little one is. But humongous. So it's a real cracked house."

"Yeah!" Neesha nudged Joy with her hip. "Cool!"

Melissa was exasperated. "Am I the only sane person here? Two little girls and a homeless man can't stand up to a gang."

"But what if I was out here too, Mel?"

Melissa took his arm. "Gregory, do you think visible presence means anything to men like this? They're gangsters."

"They're ashamed." Dimitrios got up and brushed at his orange pants.

"Fine," said Joy's mother. "They're ashamed gangsters."

"I mean," said Dimitrios, "that they aren't bad yet. Not all the way through, anyway. They pick on me because I know them. Two of them were boys in this neighborhood. I gave Richard a basketball. Maurice used to walk alongside and talk to me. So when they see me, they remember their innocence, and they're ashamed."

"See?" said Joy's father. "They're not really gangsters. And I like what the girls are doing to this house; they're asking people to look at something familiar in a new way."

"This is a bad idea," Melissa snapped. "And it's not going any further. This is it. The end.

Finito. Leave the mirrors if you want and let the junkies comb their hair and put on makeup before they buy crack. But these little girls are not going to be out here playing with broken glass and paint when a carful of career criminals drives by again."

She reached for Joy, who stepped back. "But, Mom—"

"No buts. You're coming home with me, and you're staying home."

Gregory leaned forward. "Melon, c'mon."

"My name is Melissa. Not Melon."

He tried to reassure her. "I'd be with them every second."

"And me," said Mr. Lossi.

Joy's mom laughed, but it was one of those sour laughs. "Oh, fine. A painter and a seventy-year-old Italian. That'd stop any nineteen-year-old psychopath with an Uzi."

Neesha's father cleared his throat. "I know why you're wary, Melissa, but nobody's got a gun."

"Not this time, Walter. But what about next time?"

"We'd just be here in the daytime," he said. "Nobody's going to shoot four grown-ups in broad daylight."

"Five," said Mrs. Santiago.

"It's not like we're taking anything away from

The Condemned," said Walter. "We're just defending our neighborhood."

Gregory laid his hand across his heart. "Neesha and Joy are onto something here. I can feel it."

Melissa turned to Neesha's grandmother. "Help me, Mrs. Kincaid. You know I'm right, don't you?"

She patted Melissa's arm. "It don't help to give in, honey. We lay down now, what's next for us?"

"Nobody's giving in! I just want these children out of harm's way."

Joy reached for her mother. "There's not that much more to do. It can't take long. Just let us finish. Please?"

"A day," said Gregory. "Two at the most."

Melissa put her face in her hands. "Unbelievable. A complete nightmare. Everything I was afraid of when we moved here. Oh, my God."

8

NEXT MORNING Gregory, Walter, and Dimitrios unloaded paint and rollers and pans out of the hatch of the Volvo. Neesha and Joy stood back and looked things over.

"It's so cool we're going to paint a big crack on a crack house," said Neesha. "How'd you think of that?"

"I don't know. While Mom was worrying out loud, I was looking at the front, and all of a sudden it just came to me." She turned to her friend. "How'd you think of putting mirrors up there?"

"I was just lookin' at the house."

"That's what artists do first," Gregory said without even glancing up. "They look."

Pieces of broken glass reflected his blue

shirt, a piece of Walter's sunglasses, a scrap of Dimitrios's green pants.

"Maybe," Joy said, "we should stencil 'Just Look at Yourself' right around the door? I can at least stencil."

Neesha glanced over her shoulder. Mr. Lossi and Mrs. Santiago were sitting in striped lawn chairs. "He could write something in Italian."

"And she could draw some magical stuff maybe."

"Mr. Park could write in Korean."

Neesha looked toward Joy's house, less than a block away. "Would your mom write something, or is she still mad?"

"She called in sick, got right in the bathtub this morning, and stayed there, so she's still upset."

"Girls!"

They looked at Joy's father, who was lining up three slanty trays shimmering with either black paint or white. Some rollers—two on the ends of long handles—leaned against the wall.

"Let's get this show on the road," he said, "before The Condemned crawl out of bed and put on their scowls. Where do we start?"

"Well," Joy said. "It's easy. We'll just follow the crack."

Neesha scratched her head. "Who's 'we'?"

"Well, anybody, I guess. Not me, though. I can't draw. You do it, Dad. You're the artist."

He held up his hands. "No, no. I'm just the gofer. I go for stuff."

Joy turned to Neesha. "Can you draw?"

"A little."

"You do it, okay? You know what I want: just a great big crack that you can see from the street."

Neesha tugged at the straps of her blue overalls, then pointed. "Big up there and little down here?"

"Right."

She wiped her hands on her back pockets. She looked at the brush Joy's dad was holding out to her. Then she reached for it.

"And while you do that," said Walter, "the rest of us'll just slap a nice white coat on the rest of the place."

He and Dimitrios and Gregory each took a roller and some paint and disappeared around the side of the house.

"I'll go out to the curb," Joy said. "And guide you, okay?"

She backed down the sidewalk until she got to the street. Behind her was the surfy sound of cars and trucks passing. She watched Neesha dip her clean brush into the black paint and start to make the first jagged line.

She was pretty good. She only stopped once and looked back. Joy raised her thumb, signaling okay.

When a car pulled up behind her and its brakes squealed, she froze.

"What are you doin', child?"

Joy turned around to see a brown UPS truck. Its driver stood in the door.

"We're making a cracked house."

The lady scowled. "What do you mean, you're making a crack house."

"Crack*ed*." She emphasized the last two letters. Then she pointed. "See?"

The driver looked at her intently. "You live in this neighborhood?"

"Yes, ma'am. Do you?"

"Not too far." She waved toward the ocean. She shaded her eyes as Gregory and Walter came around from behind the house, then squatted beside the stacked cans of paint. One drank from a water bottle, then passed it to the other, who drank and poured some on his head.

"These your people?"

"My dad, and my friend's dad, and our friend Dimitrios."

A loud, cranky horn made the driver jump back into her truck and turn the key. "See you guys later," she said. "I'm not sure what you all are up to, but I like it. And I'll be watching."

There were grown-ups working, and the house was little, anyway, so the painting went fast. By noon, the back and the sides were almost dry.

Dimitrios held Neesha on his shoulders while she finished up. The others stood back by the curb.

"Piece of cake," said Joy's father. "I'll do a little close work here and there, and that'll be that."

"Then maybe," said Walter, "your wife will get out of the tub."

"I hope she didn't shrink. I don't want to have to buy her all new clothes."

"You didn't check before you married her? Man, you have to think ahead. They're not pre-shrunk, don't even think of hauling that ring out."

Joy listened to them laugh. "That's grown-up stuff, isn't it." She turned to Neesha. "I never get grown-up stuff."

"I bet we're not missing much."

That's when they heard it. The heavy *thud-shunka-shunka-shunka-thunk* of huge speakers. They looked at one another.

"You girls go with Dimitrios," said Walter.

He and Gregory stood shoulder to shoulder; then they turned and walked to the curb.

The window of the Chevrolet dropped like a guillotine.

"I thought," said a voice from the gloom, "we told you all who this house belong to now."

"Don't do anything stupid," said Walter.

"What you doin' standin' up side Whitey, any-way." It was the no-neck boy, frowning again.

"It's a flaw in my nature to like decent people; write me off as a hopeless case." Then Neesha's father leaned forward. "Your dad was a decent man, Richard. You were a good kid. What happened? Why are you in this car? Why are you acting like this?"

From the backseat someone growled, "Shut him up."

Gregory, with one arm around Walter's shoulder to steady him, leaned in. "Look around you, fellas. Open your eyes and just look around."

Neesha and Joy followed her father's finger. There was Mr. Lossi and Mrs. Santiago. Mr. Park stepped out from under the shadow of his awning with his video camera. Mrs. Kincaid left her porch and walked to the curb.

It was like one of those old westerns—grizzled outlaws on sweaty horses plunge into town, and citizens appear on the roof of the general store, in the belfry of the church, and from behind the watering trough. Except this time the citizens didn't have guns. They had cell phones and camcorders.

"We've got your license number already," said Walter. "I know most of your names. Anything you do today or from now on we'll get on tape."

"So get smart," Gregory said. "Move on. Leave Ibarra Street alone. Take your nasty business somewhere else."

Neesha nudged Joy, and they ran halfway

down the walk and screamed at the car, "Yeah, get out of here. Scram."

"This ain't finished!" said a deep voice.

"That's right," Gregory said, "but it will be in an hour or so."

The window shot up, the car patched out. Gregory and Walter sagged against each other. Each put one limp arm around the girls.

"Scram?" Gregory said. "What have you been reading?"

"They left, didn't they?" said Joy.

"Oh yeah. Right," said Walter. "They were probably scared of that bear on your shirt."

Mr. Park came from across the street. He shook hands with Mrs. Santiago. Mr. Lossi was grinning. He started shaking everybody's hand.

"You go back to work," he said. "We'll stand guard."

"I stay too," said Mr. Park. "Not just watch. My wife can handle store."

Neesha's grandmother said she'd get some things to snack on. "It's past noon. You can't paint on an empty stomach."

Finishing up didn't take long at all. And, anyway, now more people were painting or touching up or raking or standing guard or opening cold drinks. When Joy looked up the street, she could see her mom watching from the upstairs window.

By two o'clock, they were done. Joy stood on the sidewalk and admired the house—the spooky-looking scar, the glittering arch around the door, the fresh paint everywhere. The house seemed to stand up straighter.

She was grinning at everyone when a police cruiser pulled up to the curb. Two officers, black and white like their car, got out. They ran their hands over their batons. They hitched up their heavy revolvers.

"Glad you could make it." Mr. Lossi's voice was raspier than usual. "But the party was yesterday."

"This house belong to you?" asked the white police officer, looking at Gregory.

Joy could see her father read the silver name tag that hung on the dark blue shirt.

"Well, Officer Kennison," he said amiably. "No, it isn't exactly mine."

"Somebody's got to own it." This was the other police officer, Officer Hamby.

"I suppose that's true," said Gregory. "But I doubt if he'd mind that we painted it."

"Bottom line," said Officer Hamby, "is this— it's not your property."

Neesha stepped up beside her father. "But we did it to keep the crack dealers away."

"What crack dealers?" Officer Kennison pointed to Dimitrios. "Are you dealing crack?"

"That's right," said Mrs. Santiago. "Pick on the black man."

"And who are you, lady?"

"Look," said Joy. "You don't understand. Some of those Condemned guys were almost for sure going to turn this into a crack house, so Neesha and I started to kind of fix it up and stuff."

Officer Kennison took off his hat and reached for his ticket book. "But you didn't fix it up. You made a spectacle out of somebody else's property!"

Joy grinned at Neesha. "That's right!" She tugged at her father. "It *is* a spectacle."

"*That's* what it needed!" said Neesha. "Spectacle-ness." She took Officer Hamby's hand and turned him toward the busy street, where cars were slowing down to take in the scene. "No way those *criminales* are gonna sell drugs with everybody starin' at their house."

"I don't see any criminals," said Officer Kennison. "All I see is a bunch of people trespassing."

Mr. Park's eyes were bulging. "Trespassing? Where trespassing when people stealing from me?"

Officer Hamby got out his book too. "You want me to add unlawful assembly to trespassing and vandalism?"

Mr. Park raised his camcorder and started filming. Mrs. Kincaid said she knew Officer Hamby's mother and why didn't he call her more or stop by, the poor thing. Dimitrios started to drift away. Mr. Lossi was muttering about the mayor and trying to dial his cell phone.

Just then Neesha nudged Joy, and they watched Melissa steam past the muffler shop and right into the center of the storm.

"Everybody! Everybody! I have good news. I just talked to Josh at the gallery, and he says that even though this project is site specific, he'll still sponsor it."

Everyone looked at everyone else, then at Melissa.

"So," she announced, "the opening is August twelfth." She smiled at both police officers. "You're invited."

Officer Hamby moved closer to Joy's mother. "Do you own this place?"

"Oh, no. The house belongs to Mr. Orozco. I'm just the artists' mother." One arm went around Joy, the other around Neesha.

Officer Hamby's eyes got real narrow. "These here kids are artists?"

Melissa nodded. "And Mr. Orozco loves the title of this piece, by the way."

Everyone looked at Melissa again. She looked down at Joy.

"Want to tell them what it is, sweetheart?"

"The title? Uh, no. You go ahead, Mom."

"Neesha?"

"Uh, no. You go ahead, Mom."

"Well, it's called *The Heart of the City*."

Nobody said anything. They just looked at the house, at one another, at Melissa. Then they nodded. Finally Officer Kennison said, "You're sure you have the owner's permission here."

"Absolutely." Melissa looked up at each police officer. "And don't forget to come to the opening. Bring your families."

The officers glanced at each other, then at the house. One of them looked right at Melissa. "Just for the record," he said, "who belongs to who here? I mean, where are these little girls' parents?"

"Right here," said Melissa.

"They're yours? But one of them's . . ."

Walter stepped forward. "Actually, they're mine."

"So you two are married?"

"Nope."

"They're mine," said Mr. Lossi.

Mrs. Santiago drew the girls into her wide skirts. "And mine."

"Our girls too," said Mr. Park.

The officers just looked at each other. Behind them, their car radio crackled. They shrugged and put away their ticket books.

As the police car drove off, Joy's mother waved good-bye, then turned right into her husband, who had his arms spread wide.

Mrs. Kincaid hugged her too. Mr. Lossi took her hand. Mrs. Santiago put both arms around her. Walter kissed Melissa's cheek. Neesha and Joy hung on her arms. Dimitrios solemnly shook hands.

"The Heart of the City," said Joy. "That is so cool. How'd you think of that, Mom?"

She shrugged. "I was looking out the window at you guys, and I just started to smile. I didn't want to like it here, but I do. Ibarra Street just won my heart."

Gregory put one arm around his wife, leaned, and kissed her on the forehead. "Did you really talk to Josh down at the gallery?"

"No, but we should."

"I think I remember Mr. Orozco," said Mr. Lossi.

"I wouldn't doubt it. He lived here ages ago. He's retired now, and he's alone. He can't keep things up like he used to. He's really grateful to us for painting his house."

"How did you find him?"

"The county assessor. I don't work downtown for nothing. I have friends in the right places."

Gregory kissed her again. "I am so glad to see you."

Neesha and Joy drifted up the walk, toward the house.

"It looks pretty good," said Joy. "Don't you think?"

"Uh-huh."

It was the way she said it that made Joy ask, "But?"

"Girls!" Melissa waved. "We're all going to our place for iced tea."

Inside, Gregory unpacked Snapple and ice, and Melissa showed people the house. Neesha pulled Joy to one side.

"Could we use your dad's computer and printer?"

"Probably. Why?"

"Remember we were saying that maybe we could stencil things on the house? Things like 'Now Look at Yourself!' and stuff like that?"

"Yeah?"

"What if we let everybody work on the house."

"Everybody?"

"Why not? Let's say we print up some flyers about the house. And then we give the address."

"So people would come and paint and rake and clean up like we did?"

"Yeah, but do anything they wanted anytime they wanted to. Just as long as they were there, you know? Like you said to that cop: The Condemned aren't gonna want people staring at their place."

Joy wasn't crazy about that idea. "What if they ruined it? Like with graffiti and stuff."

"I don't think anybody would mess it up."

"But what if they did?"

Neesha looked around. Her father wrote down things that Gregory, who was talking on the telephone, relayed to him. Melissa and the others were in the living room. Dimitrios sat on the back steps, a glass of water between his hands. The sun glinted off his silver bracelets.

"Let's ask," said Neesha.

When they went and stood behind Dimitrios, he said, "I heard you talking."

"So?" Joy said.

He turned his green eyes on her. "So?"

"Well, I just don't want to see the house we worked so hard on messed up by a bunch of strangers."

"Not too long ago, you were a stranger."

"But what if Joy's right and it gets trashed?" asked Neesha.

"Perhaps you'd fix it," answered Dimitrios.

"Perhaps not?"

He shrugged.

"So should we make the flyers and hand them out?"

"To make the house different was your idea from the beginning. Perhaps this is the next step for you."

"But perhaps not."

Dimitrios took a sip of water. "Both are good, both are bad."

Joy didn't like *that*, either. "It's good to give out the flyers, but it's bad to give out the flyers?"

"Everything casts a shadow."

"You mean what we did could be bad too?"

Dimitrios smiled. "Let's say you didn't do anything and The Condemned move in. Perhaps one more crack house is the limit, so the police finally do something about all of them. Or perhaps some addict who would've been killed buying drugs on Nasty Street comes here instead and lives."

"But he's still an addict."

"And without him, how else would you look at your clear eyes and your loving parents and know how fortunate you are."

"You are really weird, Dimitrios."

"But," said Neesha, who made her voice as deep as she could, "that is perhaps a compliment."

"True," Joy said. "But perhaps not."

All three of them laughed; then Neesha said, "Let's ask your dad about the computer."

They waited politely while Joy's father talked into the phone: "But, Josh, the Arts Council will love this. Are you kidding? This has got multicultural written all over it."

Finally Joy tugged at his pocket. "Dad, can Neesha and I use the computer?"

"Sure, okay." He smoothed her hair, then shooed her away.

"Boy, that was easy," said Neesha as they climbed the stairs. "We should have asked for a hundred dalmations."

From the landing, Joy could see most of the kitchen and the living room. She looked at her dad and at Neesha's dad—both in paint-spattered pants. There was Dimitrios leaning over the sink in his loose purple shirt. Everybody else drank tea around the big, low coffee table: Mrs. Santiago in her cloudlike dress, Mrs. Park's glow-in-the-dark slacks and LIFE'S A BEACH T-shirt, Mrs. Kincaid in a blue Dodger jacket.

"Dad would like this," Joy said. "So many colors."

Neesha tugged at her. "C'mon. We've got work to do."

9

THAT EVENING the two girls sprawled on Neesha's front porch. They'd skated everywhere they could, everywhere that was safe—up and down Ibarra Street, around the playground, up Grand Avenue, down through part of the Manchester Projects, then past the warehouses that lined the frontage road next to the freeway. All along the way, they handed out flyers or stuck them on light poles or trees.

Across the street, Melissa stepped out on the front porch, spotted the girls, made eating motions, then held up five fingers.

Without moving, Neesha said, "Dinner in five minutes."

"Either that or she's throwing gang signs for

the Ibarra Street Chefs, feared for their drive-by barbecues."

"I thought you were worn out."

"Not my mouth."

"No kidding." Neesha sat up. "I sure liked working on that house."

"Me too. It's so cool that it turned out to be art."

"Yeah. I thought art was just pictures and drips and stuff."

Just then a car pulled up in front of *The Heart of the City* house. And it didn't just pull up; it roared up and skidded to a stop. The door flew open and a woman in a pink top and blue stretch pants leaped out of the old Plymouth Duster and charged up the walk.

They were still wearing their skates, so they glided down the walk and leaned on the fence. They watched the woman unfold a piece of paper, stare at it, then at the house.

"What's wrong, I wonder?"

"She's looking around like she wants to talk to somebody."

"Well, it's our house. In a way, anyway."

"And I'll bet that's our flyer she's looking at."

They waited for cars to go by, then skated across and up the street. The woman was sitting on the steps, bent over, holding her head.

When they were close enough, Neesha said softly, "Hi. Are you okay?"

She snapped upright. She shoved the flyer at them.

"*¿Quien hizo esto?* This isn't funny."

Both of them glided backward a little, as if blown by the little storm of her anger. They looked at the flyer they'd done on Gregory's computer.

IT'S YOUR CRACKED HOUSE TOO
TAKE CARE OF IT

"No, no," said Neesha. "*No comprendes.* We did it, but it's not a joke, *no es una broma.*"

"Crack isn't funny." The woman was trying not to cry. "Crack is *muy peligrosa, una amenaza.*"

Neesha got closer to her. "We know it's bad. That's why it says cracked, okay. Not crack. *En serio.* We're not kidding around."

The woman was breathing hard. She wiped at her eyes, but that just seemed to set something loose. Tears dropped from her cheeks onto the freshly painted steps.

Joy slid up beside her and put one hand on her shoulder. Neesha patted the other one lightly. They stood that way for a minute or two.

Finally the woman stopped or almost stopped. She unzipped her purse, which looked like an armadillo complete with woven legs. She came up with a Kleenex.

"So what is this 'cracked'? I don't get 'cracked.' "

They got her onto her feet and pointed to the black bolt that shot across the face of the house. They told her about The Condemned and what they were afraid of for Ibarra Street.

"So it's to keep the bad people away," said Joy. "*Los . . . criminales.*" She looked at Neesha to make sure she'd said it right.

"*Sí,*" said Neesha. "*Las personas malas.*"

She blew her nose. "You did this so no drug dealers come?"

Joy nodded. "And it works. I mean, we think it works. Look, you're here, right? You saw the flyer and came. If a lot of people do that, it'll be so busy no way anybody's going to be selling drugs here."

She unzipped her armadillo purse again. Out came a graduation photo of a boy in his best suit.

"This is my Marcos. That crack. It killed him." Then she started to cry again.

The girls looked at each other. Then they each took one of the lady's hands again and held it.

"*Esta bien,*" she said. "Really. I just . . ." She turned around, squinted at the house. She climbed the stairs, stared into the mirrors. "Look," she said. "He dies, and all I do is eat." She reached behind her and tried to make her T-shirt meet her slacks, but it wouldn't stay.

Neesha tried to change the subject. "What's your name?"

That didn't work. She grabbed the girls, and they sank into her tummy. It was a hug, but a fierce one.

"I'm Lupe Pedroza. *Lo siento.* I'm sorry." She let them go. "I did not know you were doing a good thing. A lot of people, they would like what you did with this house. I tell them if you want."

"Cool," said Neesha.

Mrs. Pedroza stood up straight. She wrestled with her T-shirt again. "I hear everybody talk, *pero son puras palabras.* It's just the words, you know? You girls really do something."

"Tell your friends," Joy said. "Anybody can come by anytime. There might be like a party pretty soon. If there is, we'll hand out more flyers and put a sign out on the lawn."

"*Bueno.* This is good." She rubbed her hands together. "No more sitting, no more eating. You need help, you call Señora Pedroza."

"You could leave the picture." It just popped out of Neesha's mouth. Even she looked surprised. "If you want to."

She looked at Neesha, at Joy, at her purse. "Of Marcos? You mean it? Leave it here?"

"Sure, if you want to."

"*¿Donde?*"

"Anywhere. There's plenty of room."

A minute later Cornell ambled up, both fists jammed in the pockets of his giant pants.

"Yo," he said. "Sup. That Marcos's mother just lef'? She helpin' you stop the violence?" He shook his head. "Y'all crazy you think paint and mirrors do anything."

"So," said Joy. "Don't come to the party."

"Hey, I party alla time, anyhow." He swaggered toward the house. "What's Marcos's pitcha on the wall for?"

"He died, Cornell, so his mom—"

Cornell staggered back. "No way he dead. Who shot him?"

Joy stepped up beside Neesha. "You think all kids who die get shot? He OD'd, Cornell."

He glared at Joy. "Don't talk to me, girl. You don't know nothin'."

"I know more than I used to. I see what's goin' on."

"Leave her alone, Cornell," ordered Neesha. "You all the time bein' hard. You're ten, just like us."

Cornell pulled his watch cap down tighter. He stared at his huge new shoes. "Dang, I knew Marcos, man. I *knew* him."

Neesha pointed. "We were just goin' to my house. Why don't you come on."

Cornell shook his head. "I got things to do."

"Your mom at home?"

"Workin'."

"Your dad?"

He shook his head.

"So?" said Joy. "C'mon."

Cornell glanced back at the house. "Maybe I just stay here a minute."

Neesha tugged at Joy's arm. "That's cool. Then come over if you want, okay? We'll be on the porch."

August

10

FOUR MEN IN TUXEDOS played jazz. People in suits and slinky dresses waved to one another. More than a hundred invited guests wandered around with little plates in their hands.

Neesha and Joy stared at the west wall of the house, which was covered with pictures. Covered from top to bottom, like the page of a gigantic album.

"That is so cool," said Joy. "And you started it, you and Mrs. Pedroza."

"I didn't think it would turn into this though."

Around the photographs, underneath or right beside them, were people's names—Rosa, Ink Boy, Trey, Charlene. Under that, the day they died.

"Man," said Neesha softly.

"Hey, you're not going to cry on your new dashiki, are you?"

Neesha stood up straight and tugged at the green-and-yellow cloth. "No way."

"Aren't they cute!" Two tall women beamed down.

The girls shied away as a man tried to playfully muss their hair.

"You know what we need to do?" Joy said. "We need to invent the exploding hat. One grown-up's hand touches it and boom—that hand is history."

"Or the stinky hat. They touch you and the rest of the night everybody's looking at their shoes and saying, 'Do you smell something?'"

Mr. Lossi waved. Beside him stood three men, also in black suits with white ties. It looked like he'd been to the copy shop.

"These are the girls," he said to his friends, "who saved the neighborhood."

The trio leaned forward; all their hands were soft the same way.

"If you ever need anything—"

"Thank you." They said it together.

Mr. Jardin cruised by with a plate of about a hundred shrimp. He sneered at them. "You all think a little paint is gonna stop them punks, you the ones that's cracked."

"Nice to see you too, Mr. Jardin."

Out in front, they watched people read the messages pinned to the door: STOP THE VIOLENCE. SAY NO TO DRUGS. They watched them read the command—LOOK AT YOURSELF!—then climb the stairs and peer into the mirrors.

But when they did, most of them just made sure they looked okay. They licked their shiny lips or tucked some hair back into place. Lots of the men straightened their ties, and one man stuck out his tongue and inspected it. But some stopped and read the words over the door: YOU CAN MAKE A DIFFERENCE.

Joy turned when her father touched her shoulder. Her mom, Neesha's grandma, and Dimitrios were right behind him.

Joy pointed. "Some people don't get it. They're like primping."

Her father shrugged. "Honey, they're here, and The Condemned aren't."

Neesha's father appeared. He grinned at Gregory, and they shook hands. Then he said, "By the way, did you guys know that there's another angel?"

There were a few photos on the east wall too, but mostly there were angels. Nobody planned it; it just seemed to happen after Mrs. Pedroza came back with one. And there were all kinds. One was a beauty, spray-painted by some tagger, one time only, no mistakes. Others were drawn by little kids; these were basic angels: stick bodies, round heads, yellow wings. A dozen or so were torn out of books or magazines, and some were top-of-the-tree Christmas angels. These usually hung there by a wire wrapped around a nail or a tack, so they moved a little when the wind blew.

Neesha pointed. "Yeah, look."

The new one was a Christmas angel: white robe, yellow belt, gold hair. But she wasn't dangling from a wire or a string. She'd been nailed there, so she was stretched like a butterfly. Underneath her feet, in red magic marker, was this: LYDIA 12 YEARS OLD 2-4-98.

"Oh, my." Mrs. Kincaid put her hand to her mouth.

Joy felt her mother's hand tighten on her shoulder.

"It wasn't here this afternoon," said Dimitrios, "when I was showing the man from Channel Seven around."

"It's awful," said Melissa, looking away.

"It's eloquent," said Gregory. Then he leaned down so he could look right at the girls. "You two are amazing," he said. "You made art that's good to look at and touches people too."

He leaned and kissed Joy on the cheek, then Neesha. "You guys should be so proud of yourselves. People opened their hearts to you and to what you created. And you did it together, that's what I love. Forget that 'lonely artist' stuff." He stood up. "I'm pretty sure I speak for everybody here when I say it was a pleasure to work with you."

"There you are! We've been looking everywhere. It's time for the picture!"

It was Josh, hysterical as usual. All in black as usual. So they followed him because he'd sponsored the opening.

Joy walked beside Dimitrios. His hand lay lightly on her shoulder.

"You dreamed this," she said all of a sudden.

"Did I?"

"That day I met you, the day Lori came and didn't stay. You were talking about your dreams. My dad asked about his painting, and you said there wasn't a gallery and he wasn't the artist, but there was new work." She pointed to the house. "That's what this is."

Dimitrios nodded. "Yes, that was a good dream."

Everybody lined up. Nobody wanted to be left out, but nobody wanted to be pushy, either. So there was a lot of friendly bumping and then making room for latecomers like Mr. Jardin or for kids who darted in, like Cornell. There they all were, arranged in front of the house and under the banner that read THE HEART OF THE CITY.

The photographer stood on a chair, raised one hand, but just before he could take the picture, the sound started.

At first it was only a low thud, thud, thud—like somebody beating a rug. But as people glanced at one another, the sound grew. The musicians stopped playing, dropping out of the tune one by one until only the bassist was left. Then he stopped too, overpowered. He looked toward the street.

That was when everybody saw the black car. It crept up Ibarra Street. Its tinted windows vibrated. It stopped right in front of the sidewalk that led up to the little house. Everybody who was standing out there retreated.

Joy's father, who'd been kneeling down in the front row, stood up. Walter joined him. Cornell ducked behind Walter and peered out around him.

Now all the guests were moving away from the street, back up the walk. And then the sound from the street doubled. Another car—blue this time, almost purple like a bruise—pulled up. They both crouched in the middle of Ibarra Street.

Joy and Neesha leaned into each other. The music—that drumming, thudding, scraping; that raw, ominous racket; those bitter, accusing voices—hurt everyone's ears. People turned away.

Then Gregory and Walter took a step forward. One of the musicians put down his saxophone and joined them. Dimitrios fell into step, and Mr. Park and Mr. Ochoa and Mrs. Pedroza gathered behind them.

On the street, one of the car doors flew open, and two young men vaulted out.

But before anyone could take another step, the reporter from Channel 7 turned his camera toward the street. He waved for the two assistants with the banks of lights, and they all bore down on the two idling cars.

After a moment's hesitation, the hoodlums jumped inside and the heavy Chevrolets pulled away. They fled.

Everyone breathed a sigh of relief. Lots of people drank their champagne right down and asked for another.

Neesha and Joy shot to their feet. "All right! They're gone!"

Melissa's hand smoothed her daughter's hair. Then Neesha's. "For now, sweetheart."

Joy looked up at her mother. "Why just for now?" Neesha tugged at her father's hand. "They're gone, right?"

Walter said, "Well, they could come back. Channel Seven isn't always going to be here, you know."

"But how about all the people who came

by and put up their pictures and angels and stuff."

Mrs. Kincaid fiddled with her glasses. "Folks get busy, honey. They forget."

Neesha looked up at her grandmother. "Well, they shouldn't."

Joy nudged her friend. "We'll just print up new flyers every week. We'll remind them."

Neesha glared at people as if they'd already forgotten. "Yeah, and maybe have spotlights in the yard at night too."

"I know, I know. What if we planted some really gorgeous flowers so everybody would want to stop and smell them and stuff."

Neesha plopped down beside her. "Okay, and one of those bushes that we cut to make it look like a giraffe."

"Cool, and then—"

The photographer, who'd been waiting impatiently, anyway, chided them. "Girls. Smile now, talk later."

Joy looked over her shoulder. "Dad, where can we get a bush?"

Gregory looked puzzled. "A what?"

"A bush," said Neesha. "For the giraffe."

Her father shook his head. "No giraffes."

Joy pleaded. "Can we at least dig the hole?"

Melissa leaned in. "No, you can't dig a hole. What hole? What are you up to now?"

Josh appealed to them this time. "Girls, *please!*"

So they did it, finally. They sat perfectly still. They looked straight ahead. They smiled.